The
Intimacy

The Intimacy

A NOVEL BY

August Coppola

Grove Press, Inc./New York

First Edition 1978
First Printing 1978
ISBN: 0-394-50121-7
Grove Press ISBN: 0-8021-0162-3
Library of Congress Catalog Card Number: 78-52981

Library of Congress Cataloging in Publication Data

Coppola, August F
    The intimacy.
    I. Title.
PZ4.C787In   [PS3553.O6432]   813'.5'4   78-52981
ISBN 0-394-50121-7

Manufactured in the United States of America

Distributed by Random House, Inc., New York

GROVE PRESS, INC., 196 West Houston Street, New York, N.Y. 10014

To Georgette Owen *and* George Gering
for all their great faith and great help.

The
Intimacy

He reached out: there was nothing.

A cool, clammy draft seemed to float through his body from the darkness, like another breath stealing into his chest and limbs from how deep he had gone. It made him nauseous. But before his stomach could tighten, the strange feeling seemed to flow back into the darkness, leaving as easily as it had come.

He shuddered. Then began moving ahead slowly.

His hand groped out in front of him over a flat surface,

then along some deeply grooved ledge that twisted back around him becoming sandy and pitted toward the top. He leaned against it: there were small glassy beads stuck in the lower part. *One, two, three*; then *one, three, two*. They calmed him. He remembered coming this way before.

He raised his arms. At the top of the pitted ledge was a soft, cushiony rim and above that, long silky ribbons. They made the hair on the back of his hands tingle, and his palms and wrists throb. It seemed so long since he had seen himself that the sensation was like an odd touch mirror bringing the anonymity of his body back into focus.

He put his foot on the ledge and squeezed himself up over the rim, the ribbons giving quick tickling touches all along his face. He could sense his forehead emerging, then the soft, puffy skin under his eyes where he had placed the bandages, his broken nose, the scruffiness of his beard. He raised himself higher; the glow passed along his skin, outlining each part of his naked body as the silkiness dangled over him. Then he fell back on the matted flooring of the upper chamber, the alive envelope of his body just hovering above him.

His greatest fear now was that he would dissolve. He hadn't expected that. When he first was in darkness, it was like being in a room with the lights out: he still "fitted" in—everything was in its place, and he merely reached out to pick up a cup, turn a doorknob, or find a chair. But after several weeks the habits of getting around seemed to evaporate, and the darkness began to cling, thick and blotting, like a negative boundary cutting everything off. Outside there was only an unlimitedness, an unknown, and every step, every movement, became more and more a shuffle teetering on a gigantic abyss. His whole body seemed to recoil, and in that panicky draw-back there was suddenly the suffocation of being skintight—stuck right in the middle of himself, frozen, with no way to get out, no where to go. . . .

There were cavemen with large protruding jaws below him

now; they were mixing pigments, red, green, even blue in clay jars, and were spelling out on the cave wall, comic-book style, the sounds of laughter. He rubbed his eyes and was in complete darkness, though he knew the dream images would start again. They always did, hovering in front of him, making fun or reminding him of things, like old tattoos. *Blue eyes.* They were floating across the table at Feindahl's dinner party. Not a watery blue or grayish blue or sky blue, but a blue so rich and vibrant they seemed unreal. Like the luminescent spot on the back of an Egyptian scarab. His wife's eyes. She was sitting next to Feindahl, who was telling her about the new film he was producing. Her eyes moved downward, the blue peeping out at the corners; then they opened wide, the long lashes flicking the way a tip of a tongue can move slightly to moisten a lip. She smiled.

He watched Feindahl watching her, feeling strangely detached. Then when they were home in bed that night, he closed his eyes and moved his hand lightly over her face. He was surprised. The beautiful blue eyes were just hard little balls, protruding dully, "popeyed," almost a little obscene. And the dyed blonde hair coarse, like a humid, scratchy wool. He said something about the evening, about her chance for a part in Feindahl's film, and could tell from her tone that she was smiling. He touched her lips. The smile that was so charming, so mysterious a man wanted to enter and lose himself in it, was a puffy, twisted little lump slipping down to a moist crevasse. It was grotesque. He pulled his hand away, wondering if jealousy could exist in the darkness.

"You're really going through with this foolish thing?" she had asked some time later. "It's crazy, you know."

"Many things are."

"So what are you trying to prove?"

"Maybe that we exist."

"Somehow I think it's just to shut me out."

He remembered the breathy catch in her voice, strained, more frightened by the thought of anyone not being able to see her than by his going away. He could feel the trembling in her now that he hadn't sensed then: it was odd how he had another view already, as a condemned man must, seeing and hearing things differently that had already happened, like contortions of memory, bringing things back he wasn't really aware of at the time, or couldn't deal with then.

He tried to breathe, but his chest was too heavy. He squeezed his eyes: shots of red went out before him, then flickered and became fuzzy, like tiny clouds drifting by. When the claustrophobia of being tightened up within himself was too much his trick was to daydream space. He would press deep against his eyes and would see bizarre doors, or wavy lines like train tracks running away from him, or small people picnicking on a rock somewhere below, so small he felt himself at a great height, and could breathe easily within the space of that long, faraway distance. He usually was relieved then. But they never lasted that long, nor did the images ever connect up, one behind the other, to create the background of a world, where everything fits and is at rest. He realized that was the secret of the sighted world—there was always a background, *out there*, some visual frame that went off into deep space, against which there were faces, people, trees, buildings, a sky. Enough to siphon off the suffocation. But here there was no background, no world, no matter how much he hallucinated— there was only the unlimited darkness, and whatever was close at hand.

He stretched and touched the walls around him. They were barely an arm's length away: a moist sponginess with clusters of smooth scale-like discs he could squeeze his thumbnail under. He tried to imagine where he was now; he really had no idea, though he guessed the girl would know. It was like a honeycomb of inkblots. Up, down, into dead ends . . . as if burrowing through a labyrinth of subterranean pockets, always discovering new ones, or at least different areas

[12]

of ones he had been through before or didn't want to go through again. And still having the strange cramped feeling that he hadn't got anywhere at all.

Yet if he didn't move, it would happen—that vertigo. A gentle turning. Like slowly slipping off the bed or off a ledge or spinning in a dream. The sensation stopped when he reached out to the sides: everything was still, rigid. He seemed as if he were bracing himself from falling over the edge of something. Then it started again, turning gently, pleasantly, as his arms grew tired. He let go and brought his arms in close and realized he wasn't really turning; he was rocking, like a pendulum or cradle, all the movement in his body, his energies and fluids, rocking back and forth, gradually coming to a curious pause in the darkness. And when he no longer thought of what he was doing, or who or where he was, or hallucinated something he could fit back into, like an outside world, he fell away into a cool unending numbness. His body dissolved in it, becoming nothing. And it was then that the eerie draft would come back, stealing into him, perhaps the same as sensed by others who instinctively feared the darkness or the night—very clammy, close, deep, haunting. And then that horrible shudder in all the emptiness that was left. . . .

He still remembered his mother sitting there when he came home. His fists moving one within the other, pressing harder, whatever was in them so alien, unclean in front of her, yet wanting, needing to come out.

"So? You can tell me."

His seeing how truly beautiful she really was, the eyes slightly long, narrow, very dark, with an Etruscan charm, yet her lips always pinched, anxious, rather than relaxing in the more patrician poise her face could assume naturally.

His only looking, remembering when the other was known, why he had left to go into the army, how she was more aghast at what the neighborhood would think, of what they were.

"No doubt you've been through a terrible ordeal, but you

[13]

mustn't feel guilty about anything you did. I don't want to know what it is, but it's alright. You must forget now."

He rubbed his hands, then spread one across his face, holding it there, the warmth throbbing, circulating through his head, something not really there yet filling everything.

"Wherever did you get that disgusting habit? Smelling your hand. What's on it? Ever since you came back you've been doing it, we've all noticed it. Where did you pick that up?"

He had taken his hand down, not answering, aware only of all the subtle cautions she would give him as a little boy, almost like fairy tales that didn't end happily, of what he could get from women, pick up, if he wasn't careful, his breaking out in rashes whenever he had been with women after that, then finally contracting something in Japan that the doctors here didn't know what to do with. "Are you a man?" the older, crew-cutted doctor asked impatiently rather than trouble with setting up an anesthetic in a hospital room, then arranged for the cystoscopic in his office when he agreed to go through with it, their putting him on a table with foot struts like a gynecological examination, and the instrument that was to go up through the mouth of his penis the width of a fountain pen, only a mild pin-pricking numbing fluid given first at the mouth of it, then the thickness entering like something dislocated travelling between him up to his bladder, his remembering the horrors of stories told to him as a kid of the old method of curing gonorrhea, the ramrod all the way up one's penis, then the three razors popping out by the sides at the end, ripping down suddenly to open it all up.

"We're all anxious to help you get on your feet now that you're back, and maybe, as a small favor to us, in return, to help you adjust, we would like you to go to a doctor, a psychiatrist, not often but just to make us feel safe as a family in our concern for you. Your brother has offered to pay for it." Her words in the careful, practiced, distant tone she would

[14]

always use when she made some announcement, or when she and his father spoke only in Italian, not wanting anyone else to understand what was going on.

"Don't look like that. About your brother. If you haven't got your family, what have you got? Remember that. Blood is thicker than water. You were always a little Dr. Jekyll and Mr. Hyde. Moody. Besides he's very concerned about what you are going to do now. Well, I don't want to talk about it anymore then." She got up as she always did to make an exit to punctuate a point, then turned, coming in again, sitting back down as she always did, a little closer, going on. His remembering all the endless waiting rooms, "This one is going to be my doctor," the tousle at the top of his head, that tone of untold promise in her voice, holding him even closer, "All he reads are medical books, that's just what he wants," her hugging him in spite of his slight squirming to get away, the women there smiling, "You're so very lucky, he looks so bright, so alert, and my, *so very handsome*," "Yes, *he'll* do well as a doctor, won't he?" that hug again, hot, close, suffocating, always the strange sharing of something with audiences he didn't know, making him shut his eyes all the more, her caressing the hair away from in front of them, that embarrassment like something he couldn't understand, as when once he visited with his elder brother who was still sick in bed and who would do all those magic shows, always performing something for him, and then that moment when his brother sat there looking at him sadly, saying very quietly, "I'm the frog, you are the prince. But there's no telling what I can turn into, really," his face squinching up, the one others in the family often said was so homely, unpromising, "And they'll kiss it then, they'll all kiss it," taking a deep breath, then smiling quickly, "Wantta see me do another trick?" his eyes sparkling, yet the face still cloudy, that strange embarrassment there.

He remembered the dinner. Feindahl there.

Those blue eyes again. Floating across the table.

[15]

Not a watery blue or grayish blue or sky blue, but one so rich and vibrant they seemed unreal. As if there were something beyond, out there, like the promise of those flickers on the wall in Plato's cave.

His wife was sitting close to Feindahl, who kept telling her about the new film he was producing. Then some of the parts. The possibilities. What they entailed. The meaning of the film. Its relevance. Feindahl's voice low, vibrating. Barely saying anything more. The looks. And his just sitting there watching, fingering along the edge of a knife. The silence of the others at the table. The conversation finally changing, Feindahl opening his audience, still concentrating on his wife.

"Frankly, I think sex is an amateur art."

"And tell me, what is more professional?"

"Power, of course."

The long moment, the smile.

"You find that quite as enjoyable?"

"Let's say. . .I'm well endowed. . . ."

". . .Yes. . .so I gathered. . . ."

The blue eyes, lashes flicking, Feindahl tipping his glass to her.

"So tell me about love then?"

He shrugged his shoulders, yet obviously was glowing.

"In that I'm very, very American. You see it's the pursuit of happiness that gives others power. And I love my country."

"Oh?" She smiled. Slightly less open.

"But listen"—his brother suddenly put out from the other end of the table for Feindahl's attention in the sweetly alluring tone he always used on especially important telephone calls despite his singing bass—"let's not knock it, love can be very profitable. Getting someone else to love you is the greatest free help there is in the world. Now if you can harness that power, let alone cultivate it!"

"Ah, but if you really want to find making love profitable,"

Feindahl said, his tone deliberately cutting across the gaze of the blue eyes, "then you should put it on film."

"All right, why not," his brother returned quickly with a little nod, "it's the return that counts. Their comfort, our crop!"

"Be careful, that's how one becomes very wealthy here, and equally unloved."

"And no doubt more patriotic."

"Gentlemen, please, there is at least something to be said for acting. And for romance."

"Yes," Feindahl answered softly, "very much. . .very, very much. . . ."

He had watched Feindahl, then looked at his brother's wife; she said nothing, then turned toward her husband and the other guests, then looked back at him, turning away quickly toward his wife, and back to Feindahl. They were all smiling sociably. The looks still going around the table. He wondered whose benefit it had all been for.

There was a pause.

"So you are a philosopher?"

"No, not really, not by birth."

He pressed his thumb down, feeling the edge of the blade. His wife just smiling. . . .

The sweat suddenly pouring out over his body. He struggled to turn over in the darkness, bunching up to have all his weight press down on him. Then he raised himself to his knuckles and crawled along the flooring, pressing his fingers down deep until he could feel the pain spreading up through his arms, beginning to calm him, fill him, making him seem human again from whatever he had lost in whatever he had done. . . .

A FLUTTER went through her.

Everything quiet, still.

She listened carefully, but heard nothing. Sometimes that worried her more.

Usually she could tell where he was from the sounds that echoed through the darkness. A creaking, a quick snap as if something had slapped back against a wall. Or brushing, scratching sounds. Once there had been a loud shaking like a metallic thunder roll that she was even aware of vibrating in the air around her—it frightened her that he might have fallen from one of the levels—but then after a silence there were other sounds and she knew he was all right.

He never called out or made that strange moaning anymore, like the first time she had found him when they were still at the boarding house. She had been in one of the rooms cleaning and heard a sandy, muffled sound like someone dragging around an old sack. At first she had thought it came from the ceiling, but then there was a groan much closer—very low and drawn out, like a growl from a trapped, frightened animal or the deep, raspy gasps of an old person about to die.

She had gone to the adjoining door, opening it slightly. A man lay on the floor in front of her with a large black gargoyle blindfold on his face that made him seem like an enormous fly. His clothes were ruffled and dirty, his body lithe and very twisted, tangling all the more as he dragged himself awkwardly along the floor toward her, making a moaning sound that seemed like a kind of low, tortured breathing.

She opened the door wide and was about to rush in to help. But suddenly he stopped dragging himself and picked up a box that he began fondling, putting his hands in and out of, as though trying to get something from it, or to examine it. His moaning had stopped. She looked around the room: there were all kinds of things, odd things—a bicycle tire, cork balls, a teddy bear, underclothes, an old meat grinder, a pump—scattered about the floor like boxes of junk that had just been thrown over.

She tiptoed into the room. He didn't hear, or pay any attention if he had. He went on handling the box for a while, probing it between his fingers, casting it aside, picking up a cashmere scarf that he began stroking tenderly. Then he started dragging himself again—in a curious sideward crawl, almost more like a swimming stroke along the floor—over along the other things in the room. He seemed to touch

[20]

everything, piling different objects together, arranging them eagerly, stuffing them, then leaving the pile and dragging himself around in a circle to come back to it again, touching, fingering, stroking it all over again. Then he left it, and moved across the floor to another pile and began arranging the things in it eagerly like forming some huge cocoon.

She was both bewildered and fascinated by the meaningless intensity. She wondered what he was doing there. He was much older—perhaps in his early or middle thirties—than the other students at the boarding house, and seemed so bizarre and eccentric, or sick, that it was hardly the kind of person her father would invite in and let stay, even if it were the empty time of summer.

"Who is he?" she asked him.

"He'll be here for a while."

"What's wrong with him?"

"I want you to bring his food up to him."

"But why is he wearing that blindfold?" Her father turned away, never quite having looked at her. She sensed the uneasiness of his shadow, and was quiet.

Until those sounds stopped she would lie awake at night in the attic listening. A shuffling. . .a scratching. . .the moans . . . sometimes a nervous pacing. . . .It seemed to her like the Count of Monte Cristo working away endlessly in his cell, storing the sand. She wondered where he was going, or what he would find. . . .In the morning she brought in other things, not really knowing why. She would open the door softly and go into the room with her mother's old costumes, leaving them on the floor in front of him. He never spoke. He would just discover the sequins or lace or boa feathers, exploring them for a long time, then combine them with the other things he had on the floor, never seeming to question where they had come from.

Once, when he was shuffling across the room, he moved right past her, then paused. She saw his lips beginning to move, but stop. He reached out: both hands came toward her very slowly. She stood still. One touched her cheek, pulling back slightly. It hovered for a second; then both closed lightly on her cheeks, moving softly along her forehead, by her nose. She had closed her eyes; her face had never felt like that before. . . .

Her mother would make her body feel that way. After the workout in the attic, where her mother had a studio and would give her dance lessons, she would climb into her bed that was in the little room off the studio and wait for her mother to come to her for a rubdown. Her hands were small, her mother's, hardly ever seeming to press or pinch much then. It was more like a casual breeze playing around her neck, then moving in easily over her shoulders, along her waist, down to the tender incurve of her feet. When she massaged her legs they became alive, with a special warm tingle, each muscle plucked and relaxed, as though her mother were playing some melancholy instrument. Sometimes she would touch different parts of her at the same time, delicately yet firmly, and then there might be a sudden feeling of bending, of being doubled up, as if her mother wanted to form her into something else, though she never spoke about it.

She remembered seeing her dance once; she seemed to have no weight. It was in *Giselle*. She was sitting in the orchestra pit next to a cellist and when she saw her mother leap from that angle, she appeared to go up like a magical being, never quite coming down. It seemed she despised the ground, as if everything she did, every movement, was a denial of it. Even her hands were usually held out gracefully curled, her fingers slightly apart, the lines pointing away from earth, like leaves that refuse to fall. . . . That was the only time she had really seen her dance, except in the studio. Then she disappeared; she remembered herself being only eleven or twelve, not really knowing why her mother had left. She had guessed, though, from the way her father spoke and the fact that she never came back that it would be forever. . . .

[22]

She leaned forward now. Listening. It was still quiet. She twined her arms around one another, then slid them apart gently, opening them wide. She could feel the long stretching movement along her back and the growing weight of her breasts, warm and heavy. Her shoulders seemed to rub softly, with that easy, supple gait of a cat stalking something; and her toes curling, giving that slight little tugging in her loins. It was so easy, free, so different from when anyone would look at her, or stare, making her become always so awkward and exposed, realizing all that they must be thinking. But in the darkness it was suddenly exciting to her how she could discover the subtle rhythms, the tiny, delicate flow of her body.

Sometimes at night at home she would lie at the foot of her bed and look out the window over the roof of the house next door and watch the sky. And though there was often the sense that lightning would strike or a rainstorm suddenly come, stars were usually out, pebbly along the darkness, glistening. She would sometimes make believe they were all numbered like those drawing books she had had as a child and would draw lines connecting them up to see what different things she could find, wondering how many countless things had been found in the sky all the thousands of years before, with the same starry points, like a dream stuff everyone shared in common, all linked in their own way.

It made her think suddenly of how far back the night went. All its darkness. And how all the changes took place in the day, with the way things look, but the nights always the same. Wherever she had gone with her father, the *pensions*, the hotels, the same darkness was always there, as if it could spin all the way back in time, reaching perhaps even before her like some endless fabric swaddling back to Eden. Or beyond then.

It made her think of God. And how the days were really His, registering the beginning of His time. And how all He had created in that garden that was so beautiful was really to be looked at, framed with nights that had always been, the same as anywhere else, like a seam along the edge of His creations of daylight, opening here and there on whatever else was still out there, in spite of Him, even in Eden.

She suddenly realized then that even He in all His wisdom could not really have known what had gone wrong. With Adam and Eve. Only believing them ungrateful for not wanting to share His dream, the way He could make a world. "Where art thou hiding?" The chill of those words going through her. But her only thinking of all that must have been before, still deeper, before He hollowed them from the darkness already there, the way a sculptor can bring a form into the air. The vague reminiscences of what might have been lost evaporating as they walked around that garden with Him, His getting them to name His things, making them look, as if it were theirs, telling them what else He would make, other things. And yet the dreamy chill of stars still left at night.

It like that now, an odd shiveriness all against the different parts of her coming through the veil of her body in the darkness like deeper feelings. Her remembering once in one of her father's books on ancient Egypt how she had seen a picture of the sky as a woman suspended over the earth, the different parts of the blue body flowing together like a tapestry of white beauty marks, the rings around the nipples gleaming, the lights aglow in the northern arch over her loins. It had gone all through her, and she would imagine, with the room lights out and waiting, how maybe her own body could slowly peep through like that, the faint points of it like the deep clusters in a sky that could outline it, even like the glow on the face of her watch, all its constellations linking to become some newer skin, some other time. . . .

She began moving ahead, listening for him all the more.

Everything still quiet.

An inner bubble of warmth expanding along her stomach and between her breasts, a breeze beginning to ripple over her

[24]

body, very cool and crisp, as in those still moments after a sudden spring rain.

It made her think of when the lights had gone out in the city, her taking a shower, fumbling to turn off the faucet and instead turning on the cold. It was very odd. At one point as the waters mixed in the darkness it was suddenly like spring all around her—that same gentle coolness, alive, alert, more like a friendly little kiss at the nape of her neck. She played with the faucets the whole time the lights were out, finding the way to make seasons come and go—cold, marrow-chilling, then hot, muggy, tropical, and one with that almost no-temperature warmth that seemed to blend with her body, like a strange, lulling day waiting for something to happen.

She felt that way now moving through the darkness, the different breezes mixing, the muscles along her back, warm and long and easy, preening as if to create that special, open tenderness of an Indian summer and the spell it might bring, knowing now somehow deep within her body the magic and mysteriousness of being there all alone with him, whatever he might do, or was doing, and whatever her father might think. . . .

THE LEDGE broadened, opening onto an-other chamber.

He kept crawling along very slowly, wondering how far he had gone.

He hadn't come this way before. The ground was warmer, more resilient. There were shallow, uneven grooves and pockets, with funny-shaped ridges that began to flow from one to the other. It seemed like the bottom of a river or the sand by the ocean when the tide goes out, leaving those shifting banks of eddies and swirls along the shore.

His remembering only the girl bringing him there. How it was exactly what he had wanted then, a place he didn't know, couldn't find, where there would be no names, no memories, an anywhere where all the wheres in the world didn't add up, his just following the girl, holding on, never really knowing if it took all of that or why.

There were times at night like that on patrol, the slow inching, the dragging, the leaves brushing up against him, the dirt like a silt, always talcy, chalky, as if a lot had happened there before and something about to again. He could never be exactly sure where he had crossed on those nights, or was ending up, or who the figure in front of him really was, never knowing beforehand if he were lost. Or the mistake he might make. All he seemed ready for, all he had to do, was move up close behind, silently, then. . . .

It came back so easily. The training had been so careful, so calculated. Only the movements necessary to do it and then get out, never really making any contact. He had gone through their mazes and obstacle courses that way again and again, in states of exhaustion, until it was like some somnambulistic dream, constantly moving him toward a door that he kept blocking out, never really wanting to reach, or know what was at the end of it. Yet whatever they had set up was to make him jump on cue, react rather than respond, and never think about it. And after a while, stripped down from fatigue, he began to long for those cues—the dirt, the roughness of rope, the dampness, the scaling cliffs, the ground—that would immediately set him into motion, freeing him from the emptiness of the dream, the waiting.

Then when it really came, when he was in the jungle, alone, on a reconnaissance mission, he knew what it was all for. The fear. That could suck up one's whole being like a lust, reaching through every part of the body, anxious to get out at any cost. And all the training there to deal with it when it came—because it was always there, it always came—to turn it into some ghostly fuel like an enormous energy reserve ready to explode as soon as one touched the ground and was ready to move, to act.

He could always smell it. A peculiar, sour, ruttish smell. It made him more aware of himself and where he was somehow—the dampness coming up from the ground, his legs wet from the knees down, the slime around his neck, his fatigues sweaty, rotting, and that smell coming from his pores, seeming stronger whenever he moved. It had bothered him at first, then he wanted to smell that way, grimy like the jungle, a part of it as he zigzagged, crawling through it unobserved, invisible, but knowing he was there, ready, nothing else inside. . . .

There was a pocket or opening in the wall, or whatever was around him in the darkness. He squeezed his hand through and brought it up underneath. He could move his hand back toward himself in it. There were several layers. A coarseness. Something viscous in a plastic sack. Things bony and splintered. It was like a whale skin, thick and deep, encasing his arm somehow, his hand groping about, scooping down and under.

Everything began shifting strangely. The viscousness different within the coarseness, the boniness like little floating islands pushing back lightly yet flatly through the fluid, the whole thing becoming streaky and smooth as he squeezed harder, seeming suspended, dead yet alive, like something floppy washed up on the shore.

Then it gave, becoming easier to push apart.

There was a larger space ahead.

He burrowed down into it, the flaps along the side pushing back against him. The walls were ruffled and thick. Like the mouth of a cave, only soft. Then all he could feel were coarse textures rubbing into his stomach, his feet going up, seeming to root in the air, as the space below hollowed suddenly and he dropped in further.

He kept turning, then stopped, the pressure bucketing

against his neck. Then the different parts of his body seemed each in a different place in the darkness, held, caught, jammed, on an edge or the ridge of the walls around him, like some large earth specimen about to be pressed.

He began wiggling. He breathed in, trying to slice his hands up but they wedged. His head came through, the blood filling it. Then he became dizzy, everything suddenly spinning, while his body only remained stuck, fixed, somewhere behind him. It was as if he kept moving around through himself, yet not knowing which way he was turning.

A light, warm line began rippling by the inside and outside of his body, an expectancy all along his skin, very feathery. He could not really tell if he were moving against it, or it was moving against him. There was just a thin, floating sensation. A slow pulse. Breathing on its own. It seemed to be coming to a curious focus, like lips pursed, between whatever was outside him, and what was inside, trying to reveal something in the darkness.

He had that skintightness again. Only another kind now. Something deeper, uncramping, close up, like a pillow pressed unexpectedly against one's face at night, the darkness compressing, some inner face, form, life, beginning to stir, move, seeming smothered, sick, yearning, that only the claustrophobia and all its fear can press in deep enough somehow to bring back to life.

Then he could sense an odd limp or lisp inside—unlike the draft, the shudder—of something else unfrozen, coming up like that moist crevasse or the popeyes of his wife's face from whatever was within him, very swampish, boggy, ugly....He forced the breath out of his lungs, trying to hold it out there. Then he sucked part of the air back in with quick little gasps, blowing it back out only harder for a long time to create some larger space beyond him. As if finding that secret so calculated in national anthems, like a strange geography, to hold or sing

[30]

notes out longer, harder, hyperventilating, so as to lift one out of, away from oneself, into one's country.

He opened his mouth. There was a lump in his throat. Then an enormous disgust went through him.

They were all pressed close together. Waiting. The place no larger than a classroom. The roof made with sheet metal patches cooking in the sun.

There was a small platform, or box, up front that no one was to go near. Their all jostling back so as not to, the men in front wavering, getting faint from the stifling pressure behind them, always seeming to be pushed closer, their heads bobbing in the heat.

Then the major. Coming in. Stepping up onto that platform not saying anything, just staring. Everyone huddled in that space, pressing back desperately, the stench.

A soldier in front suddenly letting go, or fainting, getting shoved ahead, tripping up onto the platform. Then the major's glaring eyes, his voice, "You fucking little cock-sucking bastard! What are you, some kind of shitass queer coming up here trying to kiss my ass!"

The half-choked laughter, uneasiness, the rest holding back. Then the making of the soldier stand at attention in front of the group, tearing back the shirt—the two rips, opening the uniform wide, revealing the red, sun-blistered back from the training. The major putting his hands onto the soft skin, pulling down suddenly with his nails in it. The sound of skin all through the room.

The rest shrinking back, the crowded bodies tightening all the more from one another, a taste of blood at the back of the mouth. Then only one, a big raw blond-haired trainee, bull-necked, rushing up suddenly to that platform, getting his hands on the officer, bending him back, the sentries pushing fast into the room to get him off. The major pale, leaving quickly.

Later everyone realizing that the first part had only been an act, testing, uprooting any last bit of feeling for whatever they would have to do while out on patrol. *You are professional killers! Never forget that!* the base signs always read around them, unless there were visitors. All seeming to go wrong with that one big dude too stupid not to react, to muffle it, empty it.

And yet after—when seeing the major only smiling slyly—realizing that too was an act, their having responded more by wincing rather than going after him or not reacting at all. And then their all feeling something else, more a hot sinking feminization for being taken in, though never talking about it. Just seeing it in each other's eyes. Until they could hide it well, even smile, while other things were happening or being told. With a silent chill that left everything else inside stone cold, except for the now keen, quiet fury and vengeful self-disgust that would not make anything else seem worse. Learning only later, when the fear came, that even those too had been calculated for whatever they would commit, no one ever really telling them to. . . .

He shivered again, a coldness all through him, his body surface shrivelling, his testicles quickly going up into him.

He remembered the hot line they had hooked up from a phone generator in the jungle, the wires placed around the hanging yellow skin, the scant curly hair silky along the prisoner's testicles, the VC watching, his pants all cut open, the identifying tiny red thread still woven into the fabric, the peasant's little boy standing by watching.

"OK, ring up the ding."

The generator turning.

A sudden muffled sound, molten inside, just the mouth curling.

"Got to be somebody there, dummy."

The next sound, like a dog, high-pitched, trying to hold back from a siren, the wired flesh crisp.

"Yeah, he's in there. He's home now."

"OK, put the question to him again."

Nothing.

Then just the cry of pain.

The wide eyes of the little boy, holding himself, frozen.

Their all joking, stern, wizened, yet troubled by what they all quietly sensed must be inside to be able not to talk.

Another group coming back from patrol, wiped out, with little things, brownish, yellowish, dried, curly, with crinkly little jags around the edges, strung out on a string, hanging from a belt, all folding the same way.

"Looks like an asshole."

"Yeah, that's where I got it."

The wide grin. The VC ear shrunken. Hanging. Like a cowrie-shell proof of balls.

"Almost like a little cunt."

"It's about the size they take too, the mother-fuckers!"

He began shaking, thinking of the training, how everything was provided, the bed, food, constant reminders how to dress, yet all the slyness, the dressing up, the uniforms, smiles, kindness, encouraging words when they were about to be sent off to where anything goes, most too young to see the difference, or the sameness, only the dimness of that muffled rage to get away from home now so relied on, calculated, notched up.

"Put your shoulders back. Never hold your hand like that. Otherwise people will think you are a sissy. You don't want them to think that, do you? No. Only girls move like that."

And all the boys in camp always avoiding any sign, except an arm around a buddy when drunk, lest someone think it were queer, faggotty, "one of those," that fear, always of what one is not, carrying over to what one may be, never knowing what a man is in the first place, and everything else saved, held in, tighter, for out there, where it could be shown what a man was made out of by all he could take out.

[33]

"Burn it right up their fucking pig's ass those goddamn bastard yellow-belly fucks!"

The blast of the flame thrower, the red clay makeshift bunker, flushing them, the bombing, kids running out with squirts of napalm stuck to them, crying.

Then taking over village outposts, rounding them all up; guys still out in the field coming up to a peasant woman every now and then trying to get away, grabbing her by a knot of hair, forcing her down to her knees, opening a fly real quick, lobing out a cock for a fast blow job.

"Suck, you dumb cunt! Suck it, damn bitch!"

Shaking the head, rifle still in hand, coming down, finger at the trigger, quivering.

His SITTING then quietly after he had come home from the war in the large lecture hall at the university in one of the philosophy classes he started taking. There were five screens curving around the front of the room. The one at the far left had an image projected of what looked like colored sand or gravel all mixed up. The next showed what could be made out as a vast number of people as seen from the air, just heads floating around like ants swarming over some open field. Then in the center was a crowd scene in a stadium, their heads and arms and bodies all thronging close together. The last two screens consisted of a slide showing a smaller group of people, then a close-up of a little boy, his eyes large and open, a sad smile at the edge of his lips.

Then all the pictures, like a sorting of peas, went off. He waited. The room was darkened. Then the instructor appeared, a tall, lanky man who spoke with a drawl. He asked the class to recall their reactions to what they had seen, jotting their notes down. Then television monitors went on along the sides of the room, flickering in black and white, and the instructor asked them to do the same thing with whatever images came on.

They were mostly short scenes cut from movies, some from war films, others demonstrations and riots, or crimes or domestic fights and murders. Some of the scenes were distant shots, others close up, but most of them with arms swinging back and forth, cleaving, striking, piercing, with the bodies jamming up against each other, twisting back on themselves, the blood always black. Some of the scenes caused a number of students to wince or groan or call out.

He just sat there, watching. The images were more like inkblots running into each other, calculated to seem gruesome or violent. He felt nothing, as when he transferred to the artillery radar unit and looked at the green dots on the screen—their all seeming like make-believe killings, as in the older puritannical days when doctors had to deliver babies under blankets, touching their way along, never being allowed to see their patient's genitals. He looked at the images, keeping his hands very close to himself, a sense of being conspicuously alone in the class.

Then the instructor introduced a young man in a white lab jacket, with short blond hair and a waxy, sallow face. The assistant sat down at a table at the front of the room, with a small black box by his hand, a red button on top. The TV monitors showed a large dial, with numbers curving up, the last three of 8, 9, and 10 in some cross-hatched warning zone. The young man's instructions, in military or technical-manual-type format, were projected in black and white on the screen behind him.

The professor indicated the rules: every time the dial reached into the warning zone, the assistant was to press the button, which would relieve the gauge pressure, dropping the indicator back into the safe zone. The young man pressed the button on a trial basis to see if it was in working order: a loud, horrible alarm sound went off through the classroom, the indicator dropping back.

Under no circumstances, according to corporate rules, the professor went on, was the assistant not to press the button. The reason: the world could tolerate only so much psychic tension and that to avoid an emotional holocaust, one person had to be liquidated somewhere in the world, the elimination of his energy level thereby reducing the tension, and insuring the general, public safety. The button would do that.

The class was in an uproar. The professor went on, holding up his hands. The class responsibility, with language alone, was to dissuade the assistant from pushing the button. The dial indicator started moving. . .5. . .6. . .dropping back to 5. . .moving slowly up to 6. . .6½. . .7. . . .

Students began shouting out:

"What right do you have to do this?"

"It's my job; I do what I'm told to do."

"But you are killing someone."

"I just press the button."

The dial went to 7½. . .then 8: the alarm went off; the indicator dropped back.

He just stared at the young man, sitting quietly, while the others were shouting about who he might be killing, a friend, a black, a child, maybe his own. The assistant went on impassively, oblivious to their arguments, simply pressing the button every time, defending his job, his lack of responsibility to change things, his family's need to eat, the necessity of following orders.

Then the screens behind the young man were illuminated with the first five scenes again, coming on one at a time. The colored gravel, then the heads way below on the field, the crowd in the stadium, then the group ending up in the image of the boy with the large eyes and sad smile. Each time the button was pressed then, the cries and protests became more intense.

He watched the professor, who was smiling at the game simulation. He could recall some of the lectures and readings they had had so far in Plato and Aristotle on moral philosophy. There was something in the words, their language, that had surprised him; it seemed so noble and lofty to him, real in its own way, counterbalancing the other things a man might do, and he wondered why all the show was necessary for what was so serious, so simple, so human, that could uplift their thinking just in the quiet deepness alone in those words.

Then he realized where the other students must be—young, protected, unexposed, unable really to read—and it seemed ironic that they could become so agitated, so incensed and frustrated by the instructions given them that they would begin shouting obscenities, with the urge to destroy the assistant, to overthrow the system, the government, business, all the elaborate word games they were playing so unclear, a speed for no reason at all, where a person who had risked nothing, anything deeper than the time of day, could easily hide his cowardice. The professor looking on, still smiling, seeming more like a moral accountant than a teacher.

The button was pressed again; the class becoming a crowd, some yelling for them to organize, others shouting to kill him before he killed others, some merely playing out the fear of who might be next, accepting what was happening, all still staying uncomfortably in their seats.

He sat very still, holding his breath.

[38]

He rubbed his hands along the edges of the table arms at the sides of his chair, the notches cut in the side of one rippling along under his hand, sharp, clear, brisk.

The button was pressed again, the loud sound ripping all through the classroom.

He felt the nicks shifting under his fingertips, the ridges, the pressure, like some nodule or little navel, springy, tense, a tiny pulse that seemed to come back in the uproar of the class. His biceps began flexing, then his hands started resonating, warm and full, a rush of feeling suddenly going through them as if they were alive on their own.

He stood up, detaching himself from it. He just waited there, his hands heavy, standing alone in the middle of the room, saying nothing. The others noticed him, wondering what he was going to do. He kept staring at the assistant, who just went on with the dial and the button, the class seeming exhausted in the frustration of having no effect on the young man, whatever all the appeals to reason and his responsibility as a human being.

He waited; he could sense the tension mounting as a result of his not doing anything, his never having said anything before, and now seeming even more unknown to them. Then he began talking all of a sudden, the others quiet, becoming curious and uneasy about the way he spoke. The assistant looked up for a moment. Then looked back at the box.

He couldn't remember what he spoke about, but the words came from outside what anyone's expectations were, having nothing at all to do with the button or the dial or the killings or moral philosophy. He seemed to be talking about a number of different things at different times, some all at the same time, varied, in a low, even, quiet tone, his hands just hanging at his side. The assistant answered, occasionally, still watching the dial.

He began to talk about the hotness, the weather, about sports, sex, the jungle, feelings, his words seeming to rub up

[39]

against the young man, going in no particular direction, with no reasons, as though they were in some sort of side conversation while the young man, a little more relaxed being off the defensive, went on with his job, pressing the button, sounding off the alarm, exterminating another person.

He took no notice of the alarm. He continued talking, some other students cutting in now and then, but most beginning to listen, to watch, strangely aware of the stoniness of his just going on, the flowing sounds of his words. Then they began to notice what was happening. The young man was also listening, commenting back, his own answers becoming longer, more concerned, caught up with what was being said. The thoughts still seeming random, disassociated, personal, leading nowhere, yet fascinating somehow, and then the class saw in a hush that the assistant wasn't pushing the button as fast, that the indicator was up to 8½ or 9 before he responded.

He kept on talking, becoming lighter, as though floating on the words he was discovering inside him, coming out of nowhere, freeing him somehow, as he had begun to feel when he had first read the readings for the class.

The professor was watching him carefully.

He went on, saying several things about dreams, things inside him, things he had done. The young man paused, curious.

There was a secret tone to his voice, a something that went beneath most things spoken of, almost conspiratorial; he mentioned other sensations, emotions, that no one had ever heard of, and then the assistant looked up, seeming uneasy, puzzled, bewildered, almost somewhat anxious, guilty, without knowing why.

The indicator went over into the cross hatch; nothing happened.

He was suddenly drained. His hands light, cool, whatever had been in them gone.

[40]

The class was quiet only a few seconds, then realized what had happened and broke into applause, the professor grinning, beginning to move toward him. But he hurried out of the room before anyone could come up to him, with both the excitement and relief of knowing what he wanted to do, become. . .in all the loftiness of language, philosophy. . .what could distance himself. . .he had thought then. . . .

THE OLD MAN had already let up the shade and opened the window, though he had tried not to see anything. Outside was the freeway, the cars jammed after work; below a small garden, and along the concrete wall separating the boarding house from the freeway, two faded frescoes, one of Toledo, the other of the Bay of Naples.

"It's a wonderful view," the old man offered. "And in the room. . . ."

He had already glimpsed the paintings cluttering the walls,

mostly of ships and ballerinas. He stared at the dresser instead; there were five nicks cut along the edge, the way killings used to be recorded on the stock of a revolver.

"...I've tried to keep a cultural atmosphere, for the university. All the paintings are my own. I hope you like them." There was a tight, aspirate sound in his voice, less from his age than from his trying hard not to reveal any hollowness underneath. He smiled, eager to go on. "My daughter will see to anything you might need." His tone seeming more like an enticement to keep him there for some reason than as an expression of courtesy.

There was no answer. He waited until the old man finally left the room, then set up the two portable tape recorders on the floor, unpacked the assortment of things he had brought with him, and opened the small leather case. He placed the bandages and plastic eye-shells on the dresser, near the nicks along the edge. Then he lay down on the bed, closing his eyes.

The plan was to wear them during the leave he had taken from teaching: the shells cupped over the eyes, cotton on the outside, then the bandages to hold them in place, a sleep-shade over the bandages to seal out any light at the sides. It had all seemed so simple—and yet now there was a strange apprehension, as an emigrant family must feel, being about to leave something close and familiar for whatever uncertain promise or peace they hoped to find.

He got up and walked around the room, smoking a cigarette, waiting. Then he went to the window. The sky was a deep rose along the horizon. A breeze came in as he sat on the window sill; some lights went on in a building across the way. He thought he saw someone move below him, perhaps someone watching him from the garden, but when he looked closely there was no one there. He had almost wished there were.

"Like being married to an ostrich!"

He still remembered the anger in his wife's face. She had

telephoned his brother, saying that he seemed sick or was acting strange, and they had agreed to call a family conference. They had come down, his sister and mother and brother. His mother never understanding why or what it meant to him to become a philosopher, considering how well his brother was doing. And when she learned what he wanted to do, she only nodded her head at his brother, her lips tight. "Why?" his brother asked patiently. He explained, as he had never told his wife, that he was researching the problems of the blind, and his brother turned with a shrug of the shoulder, and a wave of his hand, to indicate presumably the redeeming social value. His wife had that funny expression on her face, wanting to say more; his mother only convinced that he should have become a doctor instead.

He recalled being at a philosophy conference once where he heard Paul Weiss giving a lecture. It seemed ironic now. One of the things he had started with was a definition of a philosopher. It was a man, he said, who was shackled with both legs to the wall, his head braced in some vise, his arms outstretched and manacled to a stone overhead, buried in a dungeon, alone deep under the ground, who says, "I've got a plan!" He wanted to say that to his family but then thought better of it.

"For how long?" his brother had asked.

He knew how long he was supposed to—had planned on in order to lose the sense of sight enough to feel things on their own—and that had made his brother seem incredulous, shaking his head; but then he suspected that even nights were long for his brother. He guessed it would probably be past what he had told his family, but didn't know or care. None of them knew how long he had really been away in the army, and he knew it to the exact day then. Now it seemed he were in a kind of limbo, a solitary confinement, having sentenced himself, and would feel when the time was ready to come out. He was sure they would know it to the exact day.

[45]

His fingers moved lightly along the window sill: the soft paint blisters, the sharp cracks where they had broken, the embedded grains of sand that made his fingertips swirl. It was soothing, something real. He kept stroking the sill, discharging the uneasiness that had come over him. Then went to the dresser finally and put on the plastic shells and bandages so that he would wake up to the next day as if totally blind. . . .

For a long time as he lay there that first night those blue eyes kept floating in the darkness before him, large, sparkling, brilliantly blue. . . . Then his wife's face with her smile and the slight downturn of her head that sent out that sensuous eye spoor to the men around her, bringing them closer. He remembered walking along the beach not long after his discharge. She was lying in the sand, sunbathing, her white poodle beside her. As he passed by in front of her, her eyes opened wide as though his shadow had made her sense it was suddenly dark. "Who are you?" she asked, startled, as if to a face in the window. She sat up, waiting for him to say something, but he just stood there, staring at her, at the blue eyes that seemed to go deeper and deeper, taking him somewhere very cool and distant.

He could still see her lying in bed under her frilled canopy. She was wearing a large floppy hat that dipped down at an angle over her forehead, her arm outstretched over a pillow in some alluring lithographic pose, everything carefully arranged. It was one of her first "scenes" for him. He was walking toward her. She was completely nude except for the hat, always wearing one thing to bed, stockings, gloves, beads, a belt. He saw the emerald green patch between her legs—her "surprise" color—having dyed her pubic hair a different way according to some calendar of her own, to keep him looking—someone looking—so as not to be anxious to turn off the lights. And all the performing, her wanting to make love only in the light, in one of those "scenes," so oddly comfortable for him then, watching.

[46]

It made him suddenly think of all the detective stories his wife would play, the antics she would go through, her finger poised up in the air as the master detective, her loving that role, convinced mystery stories were sex in disguise, reading, waiting, fingering pages, half-veiled words, going through all kinds of secret motions, building always for that moment. "The outcome!" she would exclaim, "The outcome!" And then she would read hundreds of them, transposing plots to re-enact them in bed, on the floor, in the tub, behind curtains, on the roof, in the closet, the garage, the kitchen table, all for some special who-dun-it just to turn him on. The mirrors in their bedroom, around, above them. And then only once the words. The surprise of them. Those words, like a hush against his skin. Her head back deep in the pillow, her face very damp, hot, all the make-up having blurred, her skin glowing for one moment, her mouth open, nothing holding it there, only her arms around him, his lying over her, his skin against hers. "I love you." Like a whisper. "I love you." She had said it softly, suddenly. The tone beckoning, still. He had stopped, the pang very deep, echoing somewhere inside, the rush of something else vague, strange, unclear giving out wordless within before he could even form what he could say, would say. Then he saw the light in her face, the smile, the quickening as she sensed what was swelling harder inside her, then heard the voice as she uttered half choking, "More, put it in deep, oh put it in, fill me, fill me, deep, deeper, it's your cock I need, fuck me, make me feel real, just fuck me," the sharpness of her nose, the chin just slightly raised, the profile so striking, the blondeness like a flash of gold, her tongue coming out more, his just seeing the moving bodies receding off in the mirrors all around them, the intervals between them like the little ridges of his tongue playing over his teeth, all the lights faraway in her eyes coming on till all there was left inside was the edge of an emptiness breaking through, his breath growing shorter, sooner, everything else running out, lonely, dark, silent, lost,

[47]

the face remaining fixed before his eyes, very clear and sharp, as though eternal, drifting away like a very thin decal slipping off into the darkness all around him. . . .

He remembered once going home later blindfolded, he didn't know why. He had called a cab and given him the address, asking him to wait there, no matter how long. Then he went through the gate and to the door, taking out his keys, beginning to recognize things again just from the feel, that somehow put a veil over everything.

He had gone in the house and could hear the TV. The house was surprising—he knew where things were, yet became aware of how stark it was, how barren, with everything placed and arranged to be seen, now all so empty; he realized how little children must panic at night when the lights go out and the world is gone, with nothing really tactile around to be aware of and feel into.

He heard the TV click off. He had thought of the little knob, and how things that people turned on so effortlessly to entertain themselves or do their work were all so nipple-like, yet when he touched them now they were hard and cold, a caked roundness, really ungiving.

"Who is it?"

He heard her breathing. It was that rush in her nostrils, short, pronounced, drawing in longer, then giving out quickly. He walked closer, not shuffling, on purpose. He was aware of his eyes under the plastic shells, the bandages and cotton, the eye-shade heavy and hot; he kept blinking, a clear, sharp movement ringing his eyes in his own darkness, as though stuck between waking up and not.

He heard the little snap, then her lungs fill. He smelled the smoke.

"So. . . .did you forget something?"

He moved over and sat down in a living-room chair; there was a warmth he hadn't expected. He got up and went into his study, pretending to run his hands along the desk and

[48]

books; it was foolish to have come. She followed him into the room, as he knew she would, though he knew he wouldn't have to talk right away.

"Well, now that you have that brassiere over your head has it done anything to bring out your balls?"

He sat at the edge of his desk, letting his fingers play along the surface, moving them over the porousness of the blotters, then finding the strange little piece of chalk he had brought home from school. He felt the talcyness against his fingers again; it was still there, like an odd smoothness, trapped. He realized as he rubbed it that it ran over and along the tips of his fingers. . .*one, two, three*. . .then back again. . .*three, two, one*, bringing something else back, both calming and alarming at the same time.

"Who's doing it for you anyway, or are you using a plastic bag?" He heard the slight crack in her voice.

He had begun to talk, though it seemed to have taken him awhile to adjust and he had slurred and mismatched the first few syllables of her name.

"God!. . ." She moved away. "Oh well. . . ." It sounded as if she were at the end of a tube. She could get a faraway sound in her voice. It was a trick that she did with her eyes and voice: he had never realized it before but in not seeing those blue eyes he seemed freed from the brilliance that kept coming into focus, no matter how close, until its allure would sink deep within a man's chest, a sweetness to her voice then, low, faraway, gently drawing him back out between the two, a beat skipping, his breath catching. He remembered when they were sitting with Feindahl, how, with all his suaveness and millions, he was still always attentive, moving closer, and how she played it, seeming to swell to the extent of her audience. She would get the part in the movie. Yet most of it was for his benefit; she had begun that after the "scenes," making him learn—he marvelled at that now—jealousy, as something else, special, a clandestine, ultimate distance to make him all the more beside himself, her eyes certain that he was drawing closer, looking even harder to fill the gap.

He tried to explain what he was doing.

"Well. . .don't even bother! Let me know where you're staying and I'll send over some porno braille."

She waited. He was quiet. He heard the quick rush of air through her nostrils again. He remembered the slight awkwardness she would sometimes have, a missed cue, turning suddenly, as though expecting applause or laughter or a sigh, the way everyday things are punctuated on television with canned response. He thought of the time he had put his hand on the radar screen after he had been transferred to artillery; there was no temperature at all, like a thermos—the blips just disappearing whenever a killing was made.

"You really make me sick, you know! If you are so goddamn fucking smart, how come we're not rich then like the others we know are?"

"That's not what I meant."

"You never do say what you mean. Just what the hell do you mean?"

"What is it?"

"Or am I not smart enough for you? Is that it? I'm supposed to guess what you mean?"

"God no."

"Why didn't you marry one of those pimply-faced cunts in school who wouldn't know where to put a cock if they saw one?"

"Please."

"Do they always know what you mean?"

"For christsakes what is it?"

"Nothing. . .NOTHing. . .nothING. . .Is that clear enough for you?"

"Then why are you crying?"

"Because I'm not smart enough to blow it out my ass, you dumb fuck!"

He heard the sob breaking through her mouth, long, deep.

"Why don't you get the hell out, it might be embarrassing soon. . . .Maybe even funny. No, stay, since you can't see who!" She was walking closer. "Maybe that'll get your prick up, or his!"

He had taken a deep breath; only a few minutes, and the dizziness. He remembered trying to tell her when it had first happened—the hesitation in himself, what was coming over him, holding back—then the gleam, the sparkle in the blue eyes, playing it out with all the sly intimations, another scene. The woman: wounded, hurt, then superior, having the edge, trailing her douche syringe around the floor like a hobby horse—*impotent 'cause you don't care*, she sang. He had been shaking, after pulling out, the not-coming backing up, twisting.

"Do you know what you make me feel like? As a woman?"

"No."

"Am I that terrible?"

"No."

"Then why?"

"I've tried before."

"You fucking snob!. . . No, excuse me, you non-fucking snob!"

She was standing in front of him, her breath close on his cheeks, the alcohol and cigarette smoke, it was strange next to the hotness under the bandages.

"I'm going to go."

"Yes, that you do well."

His arm straining. He felt the muscles bunching up, trembling, like a protective sheath.

"Did you want me to draw you pictures, is that the game?"

He was still running the piece of chalk over his fingertips, then over only one, over and over. . .*one. . . .*

Her voice was hoarse. She tried to describe it, her version of what it would be like to play *blindman's boff*. Her voice

kept peaking, cracking, changing, trying to laugh, to make
sounds, coarse, suggestive. She was right by him; he didn't
move; she didn't touch him. Then he heard the slight hiss
behind her words, like a syllable barely sounding, as when she
would sometimes whimper, never wanting to turn all the
lights off at night.

"Why must you?. . . It's only for you. I only want you. I
want you to be close, to be with me, stay with me." It wasn't
her voice; it was suddenly small, very young, swallowed, a
breeze brushing back and forth over his face.

"Only you. You know that. I knew when I first saw you,
what you mean to me. I could always see me in your eyes. You
love my eyes, don't you? They're yours, but it's all gone. I
can't see you. Don't do this anymore. Don't go!"

There were flecks and flashes before him in the eye-shells:
he could see the spots, the black and white, then the still
images, like photographs seen so many times, of the tall stern
woman dressed in black in front of the Meg-Lynn Kiddie
Drama Studio, the old-fashioned hat, and the little girl by her,
with long curly locks and the little pinafore, curtsying with the
large Shirley Temple smile.

"I'm beautiful. You know that. I'll make you feel. I'll do it
all. I'll be beautiful only for you. I'll give up the movie, if
that's what it is. But look at me."

He remembered the picture album that she used to flip
through at night, the little girl, the acrobatics, the trophies,
the performances, growing bigger, the costumes changing, but
always the mother with those hungry gray and white eyes
burning in the background, and the little girl's smile, like
those poses in a catalog, always Shirley Temple's.

"Please."

She was sliding down. He closed his arms, her body
shrivelling against him, suddenly seeming small and stunted.
Her head was by his leg. He touched the coarse dried hair,
then the hard, protruding, popeyes; they were wet.

[52]

"I'm afraid. . . ."

He had stretched his arms up by the throat, and out along her face, keeping his fingers wide apart; then rested his head against the wall.

He was hot, cramped in the darkness. He shook his head. The sides of his face, the puffiness of the skin where the bandages had been, rocking slightly now against the cool, spongy substance of wherever he was.

His eyes steaming.

IT WAS soft. Like cat's whiskers. As if something were barely there whenever the girl would move in the darkness.

She brushed her arms out, then drew them in closer, the darkness slipping gently over and around her body. Her skin tingled.

When she stopped, it was gone.

She bent down again, and could feel it still there arching within the curve her body had made. Then it seemed gradually to slip out, around, as though being drawn delicately away from her. She followed.

Her body never moved in that way before, as though all the spaces were there in the air guiding her, holding her, playing against her, and all she had to do was dance along them, through them. She let herself go, her breasts nuzzling, rocking against the softness. She rolled to the side slightly, then turned, her shoulders twisting up slowly, intertwining with the flow of darkness all around her.

She suddenly knew where she was.

It gave her a moment's delight. She was like some bumble-bee in the funny dance it did that told the rest of the hive where the new pollen flowers were outside—that little hop, skip, twist up and spin around in its antics that had always made her laugh when she heard about it. Now she had the curious sensation of what was really happening: the bee carving out a space, a miniature path or map in the air for the others to follow, just as she had felt the ripples of darkness forming around her, leading her from one current to another. It was like a new sense of where the world was, where it might lead, only with her skin. As if freeing her for the first time in her life. Those secret directions all around her now in the pathways of her own body.

It was so unlike the other time, when she had first entered the darkness. There was only an odd relief then, like hiding safely somewhere, and then, for some reason, she became very awkward and constrained, as when people looked at her. Yet there was nothing around her, and it wasn't even the thought that anyone could see her, if there were some special way, because no one knew where they were. But there was still a kind of oppression as though her lungs were being cramped. It reminded her of when her father had asked her to go out with him without explanation and brought her to a department store. He had stood aside with the saleswoman and spoken something in a whisper, seeming slightly pale. Then she remembered going with the woman to a tiny stall and when it was placed around her there was a second's tightness that had stopped her breathing. When she recovered, the brassiere seemed more a terrible bracing thing, holding her back, like the baby leash someone used with her once when she was very small, keeping her in check.

She had taken it off in the darkness. And the rest of her clothes. They all seeming so very much like eyes somehow, turned outside in, still oppressing her. And as soon as they were off her skin began to breathe, expand, the darkness a cool, soothing balm, letting her move and feel in a different way. Only her panties had remained, the smoothness that was always a part of her, that she could still remember her mother having helped her on with, those delicate hands caressing them against her skin as though they were meant always to remain there, close to her legs. Until even they seemed to be binding and she took them off. And then it was very strange indeed how naked one could really become: how many things could be taken off or left behind as though they had never been a part of one, yet not knowing how much more could be left. Only the barest touch or breeze making it seem what else might still be inside to give, let go of, leave behind. And that had made her tremble. Suddenly very uneasy. And very alone.

It was then she realized that what she missed most in the darkness were the shadows.

She had learned to read them at the boarding house while her father entertained the students rooming there at night. She would come into the large living room and sit in a corner watching everyone, not really looking at them because their faces were always the same when they noticed her—set, polite, smiling with boyish grins—but their shadows were always different, as if more themselves. Some were long and skinny with overlapping ends, as though carelessly glued together, fumbling. Others were like taffy, pulling out in all directions, friendly, inviting. She had thought about it. It was from how

[57]

they stood, holding themselves, facing each other. Or which one took the bigger part of the light, spreading a sharp, black outline, more intense than the gray ones surrounding him.

Sid's shadow was like that, bulky, black, with rounded edges that seemed like the insides were pushing out, the shadow too tight for him, ready to explode. It had frightened her when she first saw it, almost knowing what could happen. And when he was around whispering to her father, she would purposely stand in a darker corner, hoping to escape it.

But the other shadow fascinated her that summer. She had entered his room when he was shuffling across the floor, his arms moving out, paying no attention to the light coming through the windows. She saw his shadow. It seemed to be turning within itself. She had never seen a man move that way before, almost as if in a dance. The black edges shifting, moving one over the other unexpectedly, overlapping with the gray to form darker, finer lines. She sat against the wall, watching. Sometimes she saw shapes she recognized, like sails, or a mosaic, or shades forming a tunnel or kaleidoscope, it seemed, taking her deeper into the floor, like some Alice-in-Wonderland opening. Or it would form different bodies, like a spiderweb or a caterpillar twisting back and forth. It gave her the premonition there was something very special happening within it, and that after all the movements turning back on themselves it would become something wonderful, magical, before her eyes.

It made her wonder why her father was so afraid of him. She had never seen her father act that way, as though there were something he could do, might do. She had seen him tremble, then draw his face together very quickly, as if there were really nothing of concern around him. Yet she had never seen another person have the same effect as this one man, or maybe sometimes, her mother. It intrigued her. But then he would never show much of what he felt anyway.

She remembered looking at the young Negro on the tiny,

dilapidated balcony across from her attic window. She watched him, as she did many afternoons. He was cooking a piece of meat on a barbeque and kept turning it over until it seemed like a strip of dried leather over the coals. He was very black. He was without a shirt, wearing only a pair of denims cut across and shredded by his thighs. When he saw her staring at him, he smiled and raised his hand with the can of beer in it.

She turned, oddly excited. It was her father she had sensed behind her, standing off slightly at a distance, pretending to be looking at the paintings on the wall. He never looked directly at her. He said nothing. His eyes seemed to be squinting, though she could tell one was twitching and he was trying to hold it steady. With his yellowish white hair and round face he looked like a short Chinese goblin when he was upset. She turned back to the window and waved.

She heard him moving. She looked. He had gone to her desk and was standing there, picking up and putting down the little wooden doll her mother had given her. "We will have supper early tonight," he stammered, trying hard to appear aristocratically detached. She saw his arm flinch slightly. She waited; he had never hit her before, or even touched her, however much she had wanted him to. His face darkened. Then he seemed to slip away, around her, hardly coming any closer. "Be down soon," he said quickly and was gone, almost as though he had never quite been there.

She went to the desk and picked up the little doll, running her fingers along its edge. She remembered how soon after her mother disappeared he had taken her off to Europe. She had never understood the purpose of that trip; at first she thought they were looking for her, but no word was ever brought up. She merely followed him around from one museum to another, waiting while he would sit for hours in front of some painting. Sometimes he would call her over and explain things—tell her about the lines, the greatness, the vision, but there was always a note of embarrassment in his voice, which she came to overlook as much as his lies. She was just happy in being there; he never seemed too interested in whether or not she was listening, as long as there was someone closeby while he was talking.

Sometimes he would paint on the balcony of their *pension*. She would stay in the courtyard below, picking flowers or playing imaginary hide-and-go-seek. She could see the top of the funny raw wool hat he wore peeking over the balcony like a cork bobbing on the water and would wonder what strange pictures he was making but she knew they were always the same. She had asked him once when they would find her mother. Her body was very curious, tight, a little swollen around her stomach; she wanted to climb under the cool sheets in the studio waiting for her mother to come to her, touching her. He became red and said "soon," nodding as though the painting was to answer for something. He seemed to move farther away from her after that.

She wished they could leave. She would lie in the courtyard, alone, staring up at the sky. She was surprised at how large it was: she would roll her eyes around trying to outline the edges of the wide expanse fringed by the other buildings, the trees. The faster she went the more the different colors came into her. There was a lightness, a buoyancy; it seemed she was beginning to lift out of herself into the sky. A large cloud came by; there was a darkness. She seemed suspended, half outside herself. A chill passed through her, then it seemed to become warm all of a sudden. She had the feeling that it was a huge shadow coming down—God's shadow—catching her up, holding her tight. The ache in her body seemed to go away. Then the cloud passed and the shadow let her down easily back into her body. She found later that it had held her so tightly she had bled. When they went home she asked her father if she could go to church every day; he was glad, and she went until she realized that she

[60]

could never find the same feeling as she had with that huge shadow that had somehow embraced her. . . .

The boarding house was her father's idea soon after they returned. He redecorated the large double living room into an old-world Heidelberg den, with facings of wooden beer kegs up one wall, stained glass windows on another, and paintings and drawings around the room of famous European artists and thinkers. Then he turned every bedroom in the immense old house into a small studio with tables, files, and books, so that his "young guests," as he dubbed them, could pursue their calling. He would select the appropriate room for a newcomer right off, or would spend the night talking and drinking with him and the next day change a room himself, creating the right environment to suit the young man's special talents as he saw them. He even gave each of them a title, as if they had already become what they were aspiring to. Doctor, Professor, Counsel, Maestro. And when they all ate at the long table in the dining room, he would call on them to give the views from their field to help decide some important issue he had advanced.

It embarrassed her, particularly having all the young men there. Except for the attic every room seemed to become a strange corridor for her now, making her pass along the walls or behind the furniture, to avoid their eyes. It was as if only the shiny parts of the floor belonged to her, and there were suddenly moats and rivers and streams, and dangerous clearings she never allowed herself to cross. She could almost measure the space growing between them, herself and her father, by the people he had there, and as he filled the house anew each school year he seemed to evaporate, becoming all the more aloof and distant from her. Even at dinner she was always at the other end of the long table, everyone facing her father. She would only listen. Often she wondered what title he would use if he ever called on her. But he never did, though he would refer to her a lot, saying, "My daughter knows this" or "My daughter remembers that when we were in France . . ." or "Germany . . ." or "Spain. . . ." When he said these things the newcomers would look at her expecting an answer, but when he never seemed to stop or ask her opinion or confirm anything, they soon outgrew that and would no longer turn around.

It allowed her to watch everyone more carefully. For some reason there were more students on the left side of the table than the right, the numbers never being the same, though one side was always even, the other odd. She noticed that after dinner her father would push his chair back slightly, smoking a small cigar, and place one leg over the other, angling in his chair to favor one side of the table a bit more before he began to talk. Nor were the seating arrangements ever the same. She would observe how a young man was shifted around the table at varying perspectives, as if putting him in contact with different students, she thought at first, and then would disappear one day, as had her mother. It was odd. When someone wasn't there she would look at her father; he never seemed to notice and no mention was ever made, but there was that slightly self-conscious, benign smile she detected, a kind of ingratiating attention he would momentarily pay to whoever was now next to him as though to pretend there was no real break in whatever was going on. And there never were any questions, as she knew that none of them ever paid, which was the way he wanted it. But it gave her a vague sense of her father's presence, behind everything, leading somewhere that she could never get to, or fathom, however much the desire she had to be close to him.

The one who seemed to be there the longest was Sid. He was a dark-complexioned young man, rather bulky, with yellowish, uneven teeth. He always sat at the middle of the table, on the odd side, and was called "Professor." He rarely spoke but would laugh a lot, a heavy guffaw that seemed to follow all the turns of the conversation as if strategically winning moves were being made, but she could sense the ill-timing and uneasiness behind the laughter that matched the strange burning in his eyes, like his shadow, and it frightened her. She often wondered why he had to be there.

She remembered once at night while she was in the attic how she heard the footsteps on the stairs. The only one who ever came up was her father when he needed her to do something, and she could barely hear his movement as he was always hesitant to enter the attic. She would listen early in the morning when he went to his studio to work and sometimes there was a lightness, a casual brushing sound on the stairs like a breeze rustling through old fallen leaves. But these footsteps were heavy, rude, and she seemed to know right away what they meant, wanted. A reaction seized her, not fear really, but a painful, uncomfortable *why?* She had seen him staring at her during dinner, his eyes thick, half-lighted, and had turned away, making believe she hadn't noticed. A chill had passed through her. Now she wished she had looked more closely to see why, why he would want her, how he could want her, what he wanted in her.

The footsteps were purposely loud. As though he intended her to know ahead of time. Then he was at the doorway. He just stood there, the stairwell making his body more hulking, swollen, about to overflow the small door frame. She backed away, the turmoil in his presence pushing in upon her. She looked at his face to see why he had really come, but there was nothing. Then she noticed his breathing, the muscles shifting beneath his shirt; it was like the expression of a murky face, there on his chest, large, grimacing, confused.

She remembered the guide with her and her father in Naples when they were visiting an old volcanic steam cave the Romans had used as a health spa. They had crouched down in the sulfurous fumes to get below the intense, muggy heat; the guide was holding onto her hand—the first time a man had—and his hand suddenly began gnawing at hers, large and

[63]

sweaty, squeezing, like a frantic animal trying to eat its way out of something. She was frightened but held still, his hand still pressing, the steam making her dizzy. When they left the cave she dug her hand down quickly into her purse, pretending she was looking for something but only kept jiggling things over her hand, bits and pieces of whatever was there in her purse to fill that opening, saying nothing. Then it seemed odd to watch her father tip the ex-German for his services. . . .

Sid had left the doorway. Her body tightened against her desk, becoming smaller, if only to enter that wooden doll. He stopped. There was a strain on his face to see more clearly within the shadow that had fallen over her. Then she sensed it in his eyes, in the way his body hovered, waiting. It wasn't what she looked like, or for just her sex; it wasn't even her, it was for something else. Her mouth opened but her lungs had already collapsed. He had lunged across the short space that was left between them. . . .

It was only later, alone, dancing, as her feet spun along the smooth wood that night, that she was aware of what had happened. The hardness of the floor pressing up, still intruding, like a large pole or pivot pushing into her, making her balance on its point. She closed her eyes, dancing, moving faster, turning, throwing herself from one pirouette into another as though spinning in on herself as some magic potter's wheel: she was becoming lighter, freer, losing the hot, muggy pressure that had come inside. She stretched out her arms and kept scooping them back, the air rushing over and around and into her body, cooling the hotness, the stickiness that was still there. Her movements filling out, then filling in, as later she found those special shadows of his could do, becoming anything, a wall, a shell, a new container. She was barely touching the ground. She felt the awful openness of her body begin to close over, moist, soft, sealing. Like some wet clay whirling tighter into the sliver of space of an ancient long-necked urn. Smoother, more slender, unbroken, a fine line, up, turning away from it all, almost like the grace originally having been her mother's. . . .

She heard her father's voice. She opened her eyes to see him standing there staring at her, then realized she had slept on the floor after dancing all night, her clothes still on, tangled. She wondered how long he had been there. His face was white, with a look as though trying desperately to keep it from dropping or sagging, as if remembering or sensing something else, and it made him seem all the more haughty, impersonal, above everything. Yet, behind it all, the strain still there—she didn't know why—a disappointment, an anger, disgust, or simply just her, that she was his daughter.

She raised her head and was about to move toward him, to touch him, when she saw Sid standing there behind him in the doorway. Her father didn't even turn; he only motioned with his arm and told him to pick her up and put her on the bed—she must have collapsed from too much dancing.

She saw Sid coming toward her, hesitantly at first, his face tightening or frowning, seeming awkward, from embarrassment or what he couldn't understand. Her father did nothing, then turned away slightly to look at the paintings on the wall.

Sid bent down; then she became sick again even at the thought of his touching her. . . .

Later her father was standing in his studio.

She slipped in behind him.

It was very quiet.

She thought of the times she would go to church not to disturb him, and would sit there for hours while they were practicing hymns, listening to the Latin words she couldn't understand. It was like a great siphon, pulling off the other words, the ones she would hear in school, absorbing them in its rhythm, seeming to stop anything from forming in her mind. She had considered once becoming a Carmelite nun, to find that cool silence, the non-words that met each other in a glance, not denying what's there. Then it seemed somehow

[65]

like the frost around the edge of the lawn, and she could imagine herself lying on a stone slab dressed in white with tiny glass flowers blown in France on her breast, and then felt the cold clear anguish the church must be based on, that had crystallized into its quiet longing for a father, and the self-effacement that gave everything up to find it. She remembered the austere little rooms she had visited, and the soft, unobvious interest he had had in her going; and then she had refused.

He was painting; he didn't turn.

She was aware of her father's tension but knew that he had to listen if he didn't turn and that she could talk directly to him only from around him. She held firm, then began bringing up things. She spoke about the times when they were in Europe, why there were only men at the boarding house, why Sid had to be there, why he never painted her, why her mother had left if everything was so fine there.

She could sense the edginess in front of her, a strange emptiness that was coming from or going to where her father was, a kind of vacuum; she had never thought of a vacuum as capable of great violence before but suddenly had the fear of what it could do.

She looked at the canvas. He was dabbing lightly with his brush on something in the background that she had never paid much attention to. He had been working on this one portrait for as long as she could remember, always taking it with him whenever they went on trips, and yet she never had really noticed his ever touching the image of her mother. It was always the background that seemed to change, the things around her. She was in a sitting position, one arm over the other, by the wrists, her knees pointing out along the floor, kneeling to one side, as though resting or just coming to rest in some series of movements.

She seemed very young, though the portrait was somehow always out of time to her, as she had remembered her mother, but now looking past the side of her father's face—the whiteness of his hair, the puffiness of his skin—she realized how young her mother was at the time, and how much older he must have been when he married her.

Her father said nothing.

She looked at what he was dabbing, not quite sure what it was—all different complicated planes, transparent, yet thick, as though a solidity going beyond the surface, with different pale colors blurring into one another, yet somehow distinct in how far away they were from each other, like shadows, overlapping. Then she noticed how the edges of her mother seemed so unnatural, as though the lines of her body were filling in, going against the background, blocking something out, seeming to overflow slightly, making her all the more flat and suspended, trapped by the shadows.

She just stood there, looking, and all that was before her was the portrait of her mother with the graceful, unusually slender waist.

He put his brush down and stared at the canvas, though she couldn't tell where he was looking. She couldn't hear his breathing anymore.

She moved closer.

Her heart was louder.

Then she heard herself.

"You killed her, didn't you?"

It was like lightning.

She didn't see it.

Only the palm burning hard across her cheek.

When she could look, he was still standing there, almost as if he hadn't moved, though she could see how he was holding his hands down in front of him, much as her mother had her wrists crossed in the painting, the palm of one of them red and swollen, yet his face still very white.

She was crying. The wetness on her face, though she heard nothing. The burning still on her cheek. There, close to her.

She was happy for it, as though some kind of birth line had finally been established.

Her father turned, looking at her, almost with hidden eyes along the lines in his forehead like some worn-out picture of God, searching, hoping, tired.

She sensed something swinging back from him, then his falling away. . . . *It was true*, then, what she had said, he had reacted so fast. . . . She looked at him, frightened, staring at the lost face. "I love you," she said quickly, and then turned, running back to her room. . . .

She could remember when she had decided that they should leave the boarding house. She had been in his room before, to bring him his tea, and had seen all the feathers on the floor, bright yellow, green, blue, wildly here, there. She recognized them, not really thinking of what he might have done, only wondering how her father's bird might have come into the room and what might have happened. Then she heard the noise, the awful banging and thumping. Her father was already there. She could barely make out what she was looking at, the doughy whiteness on the stairs. He was lying at the bottom with hardly any clothes on. One leg was caught in the space of a balustrade, bent back on itself. An arm wrenched under the body. The head slanted against the step, blood oozing from the break in the nose, trickling in tiny streams that kept branching out over his neck and over the bandages on his eyes, onto the steps.

She had rushed down the stairs crying naively for someone to call a doctor, and could remember wondering even then, with the terrible sensation as if someone had caught her breath and was holding it back like a swing, why her father was motionless, standing there, as he had before when she was on the floor that morning in her room. There were feathers on the staircase. Then the swing let go in her. He had groaned. Shaking his head in a wobbly, strange, swoon-like way, the bandages still over his eyes, when the doctor was mentioned again, as if the whole of him were someplace else not gearing with the motions of his head. She reached down to dislodge the leg, then moved down by him, propping his body up, holding him, the warm blood oozing out over her hands. She suddenly saw her father's arm move, in that certain way, and without even trying to look she knew who was there. Her holding her breath, the catch at the back of her neck echoing in the fast pulse going through his body, warm and wet beneath her hands. She sat there, holding him closer, nodding her head, glaring back at her father, feeling the odd sickness she had had seeing those statues in Greece, her father studying them, the broken arms, the half legs, the torsos seeming to jut out, thick and solid, as though born that way, only as bodies, very much there, only fragments and pieces, and his watching them, sketching them, admiring them. Then just sensing in that instant, whatever had happened in the room, that they had to leave if he was to be safe, taking him away as soon as she could, going to the old warehouse that she knew her father had, where he had stored all her mother's things and locked away all the other odd interminable things he had collected during the time before they married. . . .

A steeliness went through her. She straightened her body, her legs firm, hard, tight.

She thought of him, her father.

Knowing sooner or later he would come. Or he would send someone to find wherever they were hiding in the darkness. Or he already knew, wanting it that way for now.

She thought of Sid, then remembered also the man who had come to see her father in the limousine one night, talking, asking questions, who was boarding there, about the room, how strange, unwell he must be acting, to call if necessary, then all the telephone calls asking what he might be doing, whoever that other man was and why he wanted to know.

A chill went through her, afraid.

Then suddenly everything became very crisp, alert, alive.

THAT *draft* came back again.

More a presence slipping in under his fingernails, cold, empty, circulating slowly, sliding down within him where the warmth was leaving, like slivers of bamboo. His tongue became dry. He shuddered, a cloying all along his insides, as though something foul and alien were there trying to claim his whole body.

He hurried to another wall.

It was soft and had holes and crusty scales; they were warm

and springy. His fingers jammed underneath them, wedging between his nails, tight and packed. Then he ripped them off, the sudden looseness a relief, his fingers seeming to work quickly on their own. Tiny pieces came off that were large and satisfying. An eerie sweat coming over him.

He bent down, doubling up, then forced himself to crawl along a ramp, squeezing into a narrow corner at the top in the darkness. His stomach stretched over a break in the concrete under him, the small of his back dropping or jutting up along the sharp edges, he wasn't sure which. The pain just came—it was clear, filling him, then it began to blur, becoming a dull ache in his waist. He lay there, the shudder beginning to leave, it having lasted the longest this time.

He turned over. His hands still breathing rapidly, making him wonder where a life goes when it is taken. He could sense the pulse of blood going through them. He leaned closer to the side; it was smooth and warped, like a bubble in a cave or a turn in a labyrinth, never a sign, anything to be recognized, giving only that constant loss of a prisoner dropped somewhere alone, drifting, wandering, as if condemned to do space instead of time, keeping things further apart. He let a hand swing down over the ridge, circling in the darkness along the cool outer edge.

It reminded him of an insect he had seen lying on its back in the jungle. The tiny feelers and legs over it, thrashing and curling, trying to turn itself over. He had touched it with a twig and when the little legs caught the piece of wood hitting against them, it stopped, holding on, as though it had found the ground again or couldn't bear the emptiness in its hands any longer. . . . He wondered if that were why, what they had really been made for, hands, only for the ground, and all those poor primates searching always for something else solid to fill that loss. His hands were moving up. He could sense how strangely they were groping in the darkness. He squeezed them, the muscles tightening, grasping at the air. Something between them, grabbing, only perhaps to calm them. A branch, skin, a throat. Maybe that was why.

He remembered the piece of chalk that had started it all. He was standing by the blackboard, the piece of chalk in his hand. He had been in the middle of a sentence building to a very complex, abstract thought when suddenly his mind went blank for a few moments. He leaned back against the blackboard, stunned, trying desperately to re-trace his thinking. Yet nothing made sense. He stared at the class, his eyes opening wide. Then there was something nibbling at his fingers. He looked down; it was the piece of chalk. It was turning, sliding, playing against his fingertips with a smooth, talcy feeling. It seemed to slip between his fingers as though preparing them to penetrate one another. He felt weird.

He noticed the students. They had stopped writing and were looking up, waiting. It was very unusual to them for him not to be talking; they were used to the ideas spinning out from his mind in endless, complicated networks going very quickly, which they often found difficult to keep up with or even at times to follow, let alone understand. Still he was already one of the most exciting young instructors of philosophy at the university, however cold and unapproachable, mainly because of the intensity of questions he would almost relentlessly keep asking himself. It struck them as strange when he stopped, the light seeming to go out in his usually alert, penetrating eyes, as if he had fainted inside himself.

He mumbled aloud dully. ". . . whereas, if . . ." His mind echoed throughout his head, ". . . *whereas, if* . . ." He watched his hand: it still seemed to be moving on its own, caressing the chalk or the chalk caressing it, paying no heed to his difficulty. His mouth was dry. He raised his hand—it was like some heavy, squirming thing—and brought it close to the blackboard. He lined it up with the surface, then pressed hard. His hand came down with a screeching sound like the death cry of something young and shrill. The students jumped. He turned around, leaving a jagged, broken line on the board, and looked at them; they seemed like the visual cutouts of a shooting gallery. He became sick. "I think . . . I think . . .," he finally managed, "we'd better go on another time."

He went to the faculty lounge to rest. Then took lunch in the commons. He didn't know what had happened. It was like amnesia; he remembered nothing of those few seconds, only his hand after. He reached out at the table, not looking, and took hold of a soup spoon by his plate. His thumb fit into the depression of the backside at the top of the handle, his fingers playing lightly over the molded pattern. The curves, the cut lines, the bevels. It was an eerie sensation. Somehow the shape seemed to be teasing him, as if alive, beckoning him to touch one part, then another, always shifting elusively beneath his fingertips, cool, smooth, rounded, like the chalk. There was an excitement, something unspoken, a kind of mute urgency. He looked down at the spoon, turning it over: the pattern was an ugly little cherub face with swollen cheeks and sunken eyes, more like some primitive deity. He closed his eyes, turning the spoon over again, letting his fingers move along the underside. The sensation was suddenly frozen; he could distinguish the cheeks, the hollows for eyes, the beveled mouth—the "face"—just as he had seen it. But the other feeling that had called out to him was gone, as though two separate worlds existed, one of sight, the other of touch.

He bit his lip. It was still terrifying, that blackout, like something unknown there, waiting. And then perhaps—his mind began functioning—it was the birth of some new idea that had come so quickly it had left him mentally breathless before he could capture it. He held the spoon tight in his hand, then let it bang against the plate. The thought struck him: the ultimate reality was still touch, solidity, something to grasp hold of, yet everything in our lives seemed to be based on sight, the things we believe about ourselves, or try to appear as, our language, racial prejudice, class distinction, law and order.

He picked up the spoon, turning it over in his hand. He wondered what life would be like if known only through touch, what it would reveal, what kinds of thoughts and feelings it would give rise to. It was so simple. He couldn't imagine our existence without touch, and yet so little was known about it. He remembered the works he had read of Helen Keller. All that was talked about was the attempt to be sighted, how to turn the handicap into a compensation for the normal world, fitting back in. Never the mysteries of that dark existence she had felt—on its own terms—the things for which there were no names, no words.

The idea intrigued him, helping him to relax, to ease the pain of those few moments. He wondered if there could be a beauty there, if such a primordial beauty did exist, one that might evaporate if brought to light, or seem ugly, as did the little face on the spoon. As a new art form perhaps. Combining sensations of touch to create a new dimension of life, or a new sense of reality, or beauty that might well transport or change or re-shape or release one from all the ugliness one already felt to be real. Just as music could blend sounds to move people, and painting or film change how we see the world. It suddenly seemed to mean a lot to him. It seemed so obvious now. The oldest of all man's senses, and yet never used like that before. Why? What was really there?

He mentioned a little of the idea at Sandars' house. There was a small gathering of faculty in honor of a young sculptor, Rudy Pearse, a friend of Sandars. A number of his works were around the house, large, wooden, nonrepresentational ones. He was excited. He wandered about, closing his eyes, slipping his hand along them. The surfaces were inviting: an undulation of knot cuts against the larger grain curves. They seemed to sweep into each other as though a swirling blossom in the scooped, arched extensions of the wood. Then there was one with a hard, narrow rim waving around the work, seeming to force his hand out, away, back into himself. He followed it along, and unexpectedly there was an opening, a smooth gully

[75]

or gap: his hand glanced back in over a rough, staggered knot. At the center it seemed plastic and tacky, moving further down away from him, catching his fingertips and drawing them in. His body tightened; it was that urgency again, but all through him now. He opened his eyes: his hand was deep inside a large cross-section of wood fashioned or cut in planes of petals, rather like a giant sea anemone. He was anxious to meet the artist and tell him what had happened, what he had discovered.

He found him in Sandars' study, a tall, wiry young man, with long, stringy brownish hair and freckles all over his face. His shirt sleeves were rolled up, a drink in his hand.

"Tell me, did you conceive your sculpture mainly by touch?"

The young man looked at him; he was swaying slightly. He seemed confused and annoyed.

"I was just wondering how you go about creating your works, if you're more concerned with the feel of them than with what they look like. I was admiring that. I've just been thinking that. . . ."

"I really don't give a damn! Jesus, all those fucking words!" He turned his head as if to go, then looked back and grabbed out at his arm, snorting. "Shit! Wantta know how I really made this one? I went out on the beach and found an old stump of driftwood and lugged the son of a bitch all the way home on my back. Then I used a chain saw." He screwed up his lips a moment. "That's a legitimate tool, isn't it? And I cut the bloody thing in the crotch, right down into its fucking knots. And they fought, man, they're harder than balls!" He let go of the arm and glided his hand over the smooth polish of the wood, smiling. "It feels good, huh? That's because I hurt it bad, man. The son of a bitch gave in." He took another drink, his eyes gloating. "So what the hell can you do with your hands?"

A vague shudder had passed through him, a light perspiration forming at the back of his neck. He shook his head. Something soft and alive again in his hands, the trembling, his fingers curling into it. Then his hands went numb before the feeling could become stronger. He looked at the drunken face in front of him. Then pushed his hands back deep into his pockets, out of sight. . . .

It made him suddenly think of the girl. The warmth that seemed almost less of a contact than a pure feeling. He had never touched a woman's skin like that. It had surprised him. Her skin. Its softness. All that he was trying so urgently to find in his new art, those combinations, the subtle temperatures, the pressures, was already a part of her skin, the textures blending so naturally to embroider his hands with other things, however much he had always tried to avoid touching her, afraid.

Once she had brought him a cup of tea in his room. Her hand on the cup before he took it—very smooth, slender, more like a special aura around his own fingers than a substance of her own. She held the cup there awhile. The warmth seeming to close over the slight space between them. Then the silkiness of her fingers slipping away under his own as though his own hand were unfolding. For a moment it was as if she were still there, by his hand, absorbing all its tension, though he could already hear her leaving the room.

His body quivered along the ledge. As if his hand were moving down the long soft curve along her waist now. He imagined the hard crests around her hips, then the soft rising of her stomach. A cool, feathery inrush of air flared around his nostrils; his hands trembled. His heart began to beat with a pulse issuing in some new sense of time . . . fast, tense, quickening . . . Then he felt his body tighten—the acrid, milky smell enveloping him in the darkness.

He turned over on the ledge and listened.

He sensed his skin stretching out all along him, growing taut.

[77]

Then something rippled in the air.

Low, barely perceptible.

As if he were listening through his whole body, hearing through his skin in the darkness. A strange hum washing over him.

He began crawling cautiously along the ledge, finding where he should go—what to follow—by the instep along his back, his shoulder blades moving one against the other, rubbing, warming. Then his skin tingled, that hum becoming stronger. He held his breath. The more taut he became, the more it was there, like the inside of a clam shell sounding softly against his body.

He put his hands out: there was a filminess, something heavier, more dense. For a second he seemed to be reeling back or to the side, then a spongy softness out in front of him began to close over his hands like deep, hidden pockets in the blackness. His fingers continued to sink in, the temperature and pressure of whatever was there blending to give a sensation of wetness, though when he pulled back, his fingers were dry.

It was a thin rubber sheet. With a talcy, filmy surface. Somehow stretched out like a wall or balloon or covering in front of him. He spread his palms over it, its giving, yet tensing back. It made something else funnel up from the pit of his stomach, very swampish, unclear, furious, playing out in the darkness around him, bringing other things back, close up. He rubbed his hands back and forth quickly over the rubber, his nails streaking sharp against the surface like skin he wanted to dig into, something he wanted to burst. It made him more aware of the pungent odor all around him.

He felt dizzy.

He pressed his hands deeper into the wall, the squeezed rubber tightening back around his curled fingers like an odd webbing. It held his body spread-eagle. His hands clenched, just hanging there, unable to move. A cold sweat outlining him against the sheet.

There was a little tug, a push.

That flash fury inside him dropped back instantly.

The tug was there again. On the outside.

He pushed back.

It was a glancing, tapping movement against his.

He held still, his palms outstretched.

The movement came and went. It was small, but it seemed to circle around his hands, growing larger the more it went over them. It was like a sudden tie-line catching, as when he had gone fishing, between himself and some other creature he couldn't see, there, struggling, yet unsure of what. He had gone only that once because of what it had done to him. But now it was softer, coming closer, circling. With the relief knowing it was just she who was near.

He pressed firmly, then released, then pressed again.

It came back.

Mirroring his hand in the darkness.

It was stronger, seeming quicker, closer together.

She was still there.

He moved his hand to the side, a tightening by the edge of his palm where the rubber was stretching. Her hand moved onto that curve; it seemed warped, strangely around his, piggyback, not really touching.

It made him think of the times they walked around the city, when he would leave the room to find something, her hand inside his arm, resting lightly. It was only her wrist he was aware of, guiding him with a soft pressure, this way, that, waiting patiently while he stopped to explore something. She never took it out, just letting it go slack, when he was doing something, almost not there, always silent. Then they would go on walking, and it would be there again at his side. He was following her but it never seemed that way.

He marvelled once at how graceful she must be, to move that way, never showing any of the embarrassment she might have, considering how odd he must appear. It gave him a sense of something he hadn't had for a long time, of some woman strolling simply with him, however old-fashioned that was, her hand nestled safely at his elbow. It was the first time he really became aware of the girl. How, sometimes, with all her grace, she would seem to stumble or move awkwardly against him, or slightly behind. And in those moments, curiously, he could feel how much she was really holding on. He had stopped once and put his hand over hers, and was surprised when he found it clenched, trembling. Then it seemed to open up to him again in the hollow of his elbow. . . .

Her hand slipped off.

He moved back along the rubber. It was gone. He thought she had understood.

He placed his hands slowly up and down, to the sides. He couldn't tell in the darkness really what angle he was at; the wall or sheet had seemed straight, but now he wasn't sure if he weren't more at some slant, the way his forehead kept dipping in and off the filmy surface. It was like when his mother would come to say good night, leaning over, the coolness of her cross swinging down lightly to his forehead, his lips, in the dark.

He leaned to the side. He reached below, running his fingers along the bottom. The rubber was wound and wedged somehow in the flooring—it was difficult to tell how far out it went in the darkness, where to get across, the smallest space taking so long. He moved his hands up and out in different directions. Then pressed deeper, waiting.

The sheet seemed so cold now—just a pressure, tight, stretched across him, making his body all the more aware of the hollowness inside where that draft or shudder had been. He swallowed. His mouth was parched; he realized he didn't even know her name.

There was a slight movement.

[80]

Just a light pressure.

He wasn't quite sure; it wasn't like that before. He was barely aware of it now, like something faraway he was feeling up close; his hands were still on the sheet but it suddenly seemed there was a lot of space out in front of him that he knew he could never reach through, or into.

It came again.

Her hands.

One light, circling.

As though searching.

The other just pressing, holding.

They came closer together, moving in toward him, almost over him. Then she seemed to be leaning into it, or reaching up higher.

His hands flattened against the rubber. His palms were damp. It was like touching but not touching . . . perhaps best that way, like a prophylactic against what could happen. It had all happened so quickly before, with the others—tumbling, playing, fooling around in bed, at night, twisting, one sudden move, and then the training came back automatically. Even the sweetness of their smell couldn't stop it: his arm would shoot up. *Always overkill, take no chances. You are professionals. . . .*

He remembered the Japanese prostitutes he had been with before his return from Vietnam, in whose quiet, restrained, unyielding bodies a man could calmly hide. The tensing of the rubber brought back the outline of those bodies, very even, tight, closed. He could feel his palms as if running softly along them, moving over the smooth curve by the ribs, then across the little bed by the inside of the belly, over the hard cool blade by the waist to the other long stretching curve, back to the inner flatness again. It was all connected, circling, his hands bringing back how they had covered it, coming back onto it—like a Möbius strip, he thought, no outside, no inside—all of a piece, one surface, constantly coming back on

[81]

itself, with no real way in. The women lying there, very quietly, reserved, as if trained for hundreds of years by their culture to absorb it all, pretending not to notice.

A lightness brushed over him, making him realize how distorted his face had become against the sheet. He touched the shape of her body. It was comforting—easier that way—he did not want to leave anything in her, only on the outside, smoothing his hands out against her, discharging them.

He slid his hands apart slowly, one up from the other.

She let her hand press in gently, lightly, nuzzling in the wake of his movement.

Then her arm slid down along it, just behind the crest from the swells around the sides.

He felt the slight pressure closing in around his arm as though it had unobtrusively penetrated the darkness, dipping in closer to where he was.

He dug his fingers into the sheet and moved them further apart, stretching a thin wave-line between both hands.

She rubbed across it.

Then came back, understanding.

He slid his hands along slowly, keeping the line taut, not to lose her again.

Something brushed along the top of his forehead. It was the rubber; it was folding over, going down into some emptiness in the darkness. The line shifting, buckling, her movements swaying. Like the odd compression between two magnets trying to pop out from one another. He held on, digging his fingers in tighter. Her response there. His moving down at some angle.

He suddenly had that cold sweat and the hum over his skin at the same time. Stronger. The softness. Both. Seeming so near.

He kept his hands outstretched. He was narrowing into some vault, her beginning to move up higher. Then one hand slid onto something cold and hard; there were lacings and

[82]

grommets where the sheet had been tied into another wall or something had been turned over on its side. The other hand went slack.

He heard a little rushing, hissing sound as if she had breathed quickly through her teeth.

She was gone.

That flash feeling he had had before began to rise inside him. He slammed his hand against the wall. Then suddenly a featheriness went through him, his body dropping out from under him in the darkness. His skin tingled, flying out in all directions like a pack of cards.

He was rolling down something cool and smooth and hard.

THERE WAS a jolt. A sound.

His arms closed instinctively.

His body was still spinning. Sorting itself out. Then his legs caught hold, curling over, his stomach suddenly letting down into a softness, the hotness on his skin absorbing it. He held closer, his cheeks and mouth and lips pushing in hungrily.

She felt the hair, the beard, brushing over her shoulder, rubbing across her collarbone, his head moving up, then down again against her neck, the hotness of his face as though gorged with blood while at the same time the coolness of his foot curling over her ankle, the soft instep resting there, moving every now and then, then stopping.

She put her arms about him, giving small, light squeezes.

A rush of joy spread through her. That snugness, of holding and being held, as though being lifted ever so gently, there no longer seeming anything below her. She had had the dream many times—his suddenly appearing, taking her up to him, her letting go of everything. There even times when she brought him things in the room and would stand almost half-consciously in his path, waiting, hoping he would touch her. And sometimes he would, putting his hand on her shoulder, running his finger along some strip of clothing, but never hold her, as if not wanting anyone too close to him, and yet somehow her not taking it as a rejection, her breath only swelling all the more into what he didn't touch, didn't hold.

She caressed his neck now, lightly. The tremors still there. His hair moist and tangled, his beard scratchy-alive on her skin. She held his head closer, letting it rest along the curve of her throat. She breathed heavily, her body seeming to unfold, grow, do something she could not quite understand yet was so natural. She held closer, cuddling his head lower till it rested on her breasts, the warm weight, very much there, then leaning her neck way back, closing her eyes, it all so different from the other time. . . .

His tongue brushed lightly over her skin.

He opened his mouth. He found the soft, tiny-ridged button of her nipple and pressed his face into the softness of her breast. It seemed to tighten him, her body and the deep drawing of his mouth slowly pulling him back together, the endless black space he had dropped through shrinking, closing over, being filled, with what he didn't know, but something warm, intangible, indescribable. He held onto her, his arm around the curve of her neck, his fingers snug and warm beneath her arm.

He suddenly realized what he was doing. He stopped

sucking and lay on her breast for a while. He breathed softly. Then his tongue began playing alongside her nipple again—it was hard, firm, cool. He shifted his head and could feel the ring of little bevels, the slightly raised dots surrounding her nipple, always moving inward, bringing his tongue back. They seemed like a primitive braille giving some mysterious message to his mouth as they rose and contracted in different patterns. He passed his tongue around them—the slight breeze made her breast grow firmer. The goosebumps spreading along her skin.

She sensed his hesitation.

He had seemed so deep along her breast, his lips giving little tugs that passed through her, pulling tenderly at her loins, and then his stopping, his mouth going lax. She opened her eyes, raising her head. His tongue was moving lightly over her nipple, not quite there. She heard the breathing, like that moaning that had come from deep within his chest before, but now more like a low, soft rattle. She waited, not sure what to do. His hand over her other breast, holding, set; the muscles in his arms trembling. She rested her head closer, hearing the sounds echo through his body, then caressed his neck, pinching it lightly.

It was strange: she was happy he was there and yet for some reason she still worried that she might be in his way, disturbing him, never quite knowing what to do. In the room she could watch, here she was never certain where or what he was doing. It had seemed funny to her that the only way she could observe him was to touch him, and how that could go unnoticed she didn't know.

She remembered once trying to talk with him. He was in the room, and she waited a long time though he knew she was there. Then he came up to her and touched her shoulder lightly. There was only a tightness in her throat, a stage fright. It seemed so odd, her trying to initiate something; people had always spoken first to her and she had always managed to nod or shake her head, saying barely a few words, half with fear.

But when he said nothing she became curiously uneasy.

"Please tell me what you're doing?"

He was silent—for a very long time—then answered in a flat, weak voice very faraway. She just heard syllables making no sense to her, like some warped record playing at a wrong speed; she was about to ask what, what he had said, but could not. It was the way he had turned away, the bandages over his eyes, his face drawn and detached, as if not to come back. She seemed to freeze, then was more at ease when he finally began touching things in the room again, almost glad they had not said more. . . .

She felt the knot tighten in his body.

One shoulder seemed to be pulling against the other, a large, uneven web of muscles across his back, pinched, deep-set. She could trace it with her fingertips; it was like his shadow.

A coolness passed between them.

His fingers grazed her neck as he withdrew his other arm.

She quickly reached out, touching his hand, opening her fingers against his, mirroring them in the darkness, as if they were about to leave.

Her hand trembled; he sensed the startle, the pulse, enter his palm, spreading all through his arm, curling up around the insides of his body, so awfully alive. He pulled back.

For a few seconds he tried not to think. His body was suspended, numb, his right hand dangling in the darkness. Then her body began radiating, his hand beginning to hurt again.

It moved down slowly, as though being drawn, not of his own will, finding the soft heavy globe rising and falling in the darkness, pressing up under it. His fingers curled, clinging gently to her breast, feeling themselves fill out with the warm undercurrents inside moving back against them no matter where they reached, like a soft weight counterbalancing the ache in his hand.

He let it rock, the hardness of her nipple nubbing gently into his palm like the underbelly of some animal it could soothe. His hand began holding back, lulled, becoming oddly paralyzed; it seemed to lose itself in the smoothness of her skin, then it squeezed suddenly—tense, clutching—only to relax again. Leaning heavily then, cramping up, sinking into the warmth, the inner sponginess spreading through the tightness like some cushion absorbing the impact that had sprung through it. The fingers, the edge of his palm, his wrist, the form of his hand, letting go, beginning to melt, blurring out in the milkiness of her breast as though it had never been.

She could feel his mouth moving back, his hand relaxing.

It was so soft again. The light cupping, the fingers, just there, grazing, moving in and around, barely holding, pressing. Then her breast swelling, forming beneath his hand, seeming to shift around on the inside as though flowing between the different spaces between his fingers, squeezing through to him, molding by. She breathed deeply. All the restless movement over her, through her, as if *he* were *really* there, with her, by her. She remembered watching men, the way they met, extending themselves, clasping their hands, and then she would look at the movement that would become swollen, heavy, contracting, expanding, with their cupped hands, and it had always seemed exciting somehow what men seemed to have between each other, an alive knowing, a handshake, that had always reminded her, with their rings, of a breast and what it could be for, and she had thought during the night, when she would clutch her own, what a wonderful way it would be to greet like that, her breasts like some soft palpable antennae extending, and then to feel the grip, the response, the growth against the palm that said, "I'm here, hello." It so very much like that now, that gentle, diffused lightness of his hand beginning to enter her, moving all through her body as a slow, strange swimming. *"Hello, hello* . . . I'm here, *hello.* . . ."

THEN SHE became tense.

His arm suddenly withdrawing along her breast, his hand just dangling over her ribs. Her body strange. As if his hand were moving with a different desire of its own from what she had expected. Gentle, soft, yet tracing quietly around her body rather than entering it. His fingers holding back, so very light, her skin rising to touch them, the smoothness at their tips, her breathing beginning to fill out some other line of her body that he was tracing, something she didn't know.

He was moving away from her.

It caught her in a feeling she hadn't had for a long time, or had managed to avoid, stepping away from it in the shadows before it could overcome her, but now it was there—a bitterness, an anger—filled with something else that went deeper, gnawing. She had sensed him drawing back, his face twisting away from hers, moving down along her body just as her own was rising, turning to meet his, the heat glowing close by her face, making it seem as though it were about to unfold from what it was. It all so sudden—her forgetting how, why, where they were, only the hotness searing up inside her for that instant, making her blind in an odd way, very alone. Then she realized how foolish she was, to make herself stop from crying, though the panic was still there, knowing that the whole time she had been with him, when they were in the room or had gone out, or had now hidden here, he had never seen her. It was all so black. A shiver went through her, and she held still, her body so very tight, closing over again, becoming stiff like the other time.

She could feel the suffocation, the pressure. She tried to reach outside the edges of herself, searching for an open space within which to breathe, but there was something there, taking shape again in the darkness, the way.clothes can be, draping over, filling out from some part of the body that can't be seen. She had found it first in school, where there were always the curves along the backs of necks facing her, or along the shoulders or elbows of all the other students, and she would look, no matter where she was, connecting up all the parts that seemed to turn away from her, going out in their own space, away from everyone else's interest.

It was the edges of her *not I*, she had thought then, the way a snail must sense its shell, being sometimes outside it and yet still somehow contained, the little horns coming up, making a new boundary between others and itself, that no one else could ever see. She always knew there was something special about it, her *not I*, like a body in itself that could be rubbed, becoming smooth and warm, that could grow very old, if taken care of, handed down, polished, priceless. She believed it must have come from her mother somehow, and now, having been rubbed up and polished against so much more with her, it had that hidden beauty like the deep smoky crystals she had seen inside rocks she had been told were lying on the field, and she would daydream into it in school, rubbing it all along the backs of everyone, making it glow, no one caring.

She remembered seeing their faces one day, so many of them there all at once, leering, flat in front of her, as if someone had suddenly shoved a class photograph right up close under her nose. On the blackboard was a drawing of her—her face, all the lines large and thick, going out of shape, drawn over her nose again and again to make everything all the more prominent, funnier, the word *ugly* under it, then her name. She could feel the pain, dropping deep inside burning. They were all laughing. She ran to the blackboard, clutching an eraser, and stood there, glaring at them, her head leaning forward, very hot, heavy, while her arms just kept moving up and down against the board behind her, erasing it, rubbing it all out, while in her arm and in the breezes all around it and in the rubbing behind her something was coming out for the first time, like in dancing, like the snail must feel, that had that specialness, that other body, that none of them could see. Then she felt the coolness that came by after her tears, outlining all the more that other tiny face buried deep inside she knew that no one would ever find, perhaps only her mother if she were only there.

There was only the sensation of her arms now somewhere outside her, a slight, empty breeze fluttering through her fingers. They seemed far away. He was still sliding down over her, his body bending, bunching up behind her, then letting down against her skin, his beard scratching slowly down along

[93]

her stomach as if trying to find its way. Somehow she had never imagined it like that. It was always his eyes, his face, that she had wanted in front of her, even when they were bandaged or perhaps because so, where she could hold him, be held, its seeming so odd from what she had dreamed and always thought, even from the way Sid had taken her, that his face now could be so far away.

She seemed lost. Like in a dark tunnel deep under the earth, something large and unknown burrowing over her. Yet for some reason it no longer made her afraid. The anger had subsided, leaving a hurt more hollow than there, giving her the strange sense of his moving above rather than on her, something like the presence which used to be there outside the quilt when she opened her eyes suddenly at night in the attic and felt her body become moist. It would seem to press down, as if barely touching, yet trying to hold her. And just from the few light taps here and there on her body she could tell how much larger that unknown presence must be and she would shrink down into the quilt, just pressing up every so often to find if it were still there, waiting. Once she stretched out and let it come to her. It floated down, like that cloud, so black that even the darkness seemed to flicker out like some invisible candle that had just received a draft. Then it held her—all along her body, not even the way her mother could, her never imagining there were so many ways to be held, to be taken up. Then it would leave. She would reach over the quilt to the patchy top and press down, her hands somewhere apart from the rest of her, sensing her body as it must have been, must have felt to whatever was coming down, trying to enter. It made her shiver.

Then she would touch herself under the blanket to find whatever it was it might have wanted, pressing down between her legs, discovering how wet it could become, how soft, how smooth. Then she would close her eyes and let that unknown feeling come again, moving her hands down slowly from her

[94]

breasts, becoming cooler as they went along the warmth, then against the hotness of her stomach, finding even that she could lift herself slightly, her fingers curling, the coolness rising. And then when she felt all that fluid, she would get up into the night and dance, that softness, the wetness at the center of her, everything there turning in on it, across it, no matter how she moved. And all the darkness enveloping her like a quilt that seemed to give, opening a little, falling back, then rising higher into the air, someone, something, whatever it was, seeming to hold her there, even for only a second.

Still it was so very different now. His not merely holding her. His movement there over her. Sliding, caressing. Touching her skin. Making it shift in different ways under him. She never realizing there was so much space inside her. It was like the rubber wall, the pressure, staying apart, not really knowing in the darkness who was touching or being touched, like something floating by itself above her, between them, below him. And then quietly it would happen in different places, like patches of feeling, scratchy, light, ticklish, coming alive over her, as he was below her, floating away or toward themselves in the darkness.

Her body suddenly seemed like a curious horoscope. There was something everywhere, parts forming as signs of different tinglings as his hands glided over her skin. There was a ripple. She remembered how desperately she had tried to find her mother's birthdate and the time of day so she could know her somehow, though those papers had been lost or locked away, and she never knew any of her mother's family, nor would her father speak of them. Still she found out, guessing one day from a peculiar mood her father was in, then having him confess the day. *Pisces.* She could recall how happy she was knowing, somehow a little closer to what her mother might have been like, and now in the darkness she had that sign fixed on her right side, like fish rippling, whenever he touched it.

It delighted her, as though she seemed to understand what

was happening, letting her hold all the floating patches together. She could imagine the rest going down, around, like a dance, ringing her with all the signs of feeling, the different ways he could touch her. *Gemini*, tugging, pulling, stretching across her skin, *Leo*, padded, bristly, like his beard, pressing, *Libra*, light, caressing, then the prickliness of *Scorpio*, stinging, but not that hard, the wetness from *Aquarius*, pouring, opening, then airy. . . . He had moved lower.

She seemed topsy-turvy, spinning around slowly under him, the constellations moving with her. She wondered what his sign was, where he would rise, if she could tell where he would come up. She waited, sensing his movements. It would be there. His sign.

There was a feeling like tiny caterpillar legs playing and wriggling pleasantly against her bottom. Then she heard a sleepy hookah voice on top of a mushroom deep inside her saying, "*Who* are *you?*" as though her body were dreaming her now.

She was falling slightly. Then was softly caught up in it, a whimper, a lost cry she had never heard before going through her. Then whispery secrets, other releases answering, suddenly echoing all through her, like a shivering, no matter where he moved or touched her. She remembered sitting at a bus stop once and for no reason at all a funny sensation had come over her—a deep pleasure that appeared out of nowhere, spreading all through her, tickling on the inside, making her whole body heady and light. She cried, then it was over. She had looked around: there were cars going by, dusty old shops across the street, some people walking, the sky light, without even a cloud. Her face seemed warm and relaxed, different. She was sure something had come out; but no one had noticed. She had uncrossed her legs, sensing the moistness, realizing then where that cheshire feeling had come from, like the time she had cut herself and not noticed the pain for hours. It was strange to her; she thought of Sid, with the way he had

[96]

touched her, entered her, and wondered how she could suddenly have something there so much later so different, as if just coming out. She leaned back against the bench, very embarrassed.

It was like an expectancy that seemed to be there now and yet wasn't. She didn't know what it was, or where it was coming from. But her skin was changing. The textures rising, stretching, knitting. Though she couldn't really tell if he were touching her or it were doing that by itself, tightening and uncrinkling in places faraway from where he was. The wavy lines going out, with bumps and dots of feeling flowing into each other as though some larger presence all around her. She knew it was there, whatever it was, the inkling of it, like a shadow on her skin.

"But *who* are *you?*" the sleepy hookah voice went on on top of the mushroom inside.

It was growing.

She found herself moving.

Her body seeming to be just awakening, with puckery little textures coming alive all along her skin like on the shell of some Russian Easter egg. Then it began cracking, parting, opening somehow, revealing another darkness inside, just below the edges.

A feather seemed to enter into that black space, caressing it. Moist, cool, the fine tip of something.

There was a lightness, just over her breath, a delicateness that made the glow in her skin rise up as though levitating in the air just below him.

She had spread her hands down along his shoulders, moving them around, her palms spiralling. Tiny bits of something soft there tickling the undersides of her fingers against his skin, making them nub back and forth, giving the sensation of balancing on grains of a tingliness floating all around him like tiny stars. Then she felt him move up.

Aries.

His cheek was by hers. She turned slightly. The whiskers at her lips, biting lightly, the little curls of hair in her mouth.

Then he stopped. He lay there. Very still. She heard his breath, slow, distant, waiting.

She dropped slightly.

The darkness suddenly very clear, cool.

She ran her hands over his body. The warmth along his sides. The ribs coming through, like bevels within his skin. Then the smoothness slipping over giving her fingertips a wavy lightness as though just peeking through the tremor of whatever was underneath. He held still. Her fingers moved softly. She waited, not knowing what else to do.

She remembered the books she had found in her father's studio long ago. She had opened them and looked at some of the drawings—the muscles, the ribs. It had made her mother very angry for some reason; she remembered how she had taken them away, seeming so terribly upset herself by the big cumbersome books. But in spite of her, she would read them anyway, they so heavy she always had to strain her whole body lifting them up, looking at the pictures, never really knowing why they were bad, though she knew at the time that they were close to her father. Yet, after her mother's face, whenever she opened the notebooks, absorbing all that was said about hidden rivers and how the body was made, and what part of a man disappeared when he grew heavy or came out first when he grew lean, or the way a child looked in a womb, she sensed it all as somehow forbidden and da Vinci someone not to be talked about. Later, after her mother had gone away, and she had read more in the books, finding the long section on shadows, and knowing who da Vinci was, she still couldn't help but feel something illicit, even obscene, about what must have frightened her mother so much.

She moved her fingers along the inside of his waist and out into the darkness, letting the palms of her hands rest back flat on the flooring. It was damp, very tight, the surface with

[98]

something of the nature of his skin, very close, cool, that made her more excited that she was by him, as though within him, surrounded now all the more by the tightness in his arms like some knot around both of them, holding them, together, away from anything else.

Then she ran her fingers back onto his body and felt an oddness go through her, something reedy, a warm chill slipping just under her skin like oboe tracings inside her body somehow making it itch pleasantly from the other side. The expectancy was still there, waiting, with only a slight hurt from having dropped so fast.

She moved her hands along his body again and slipped them under the warmth of his stomach. She moved them down. Then she breathed deeply, her skin becoming hotter, more moist.

There was a tapestry at one of the endless museums with her father that she had discovered of a small meadow: there was one tree, a young woman sitting in a tiny fenced enclosure, a small white unicorn lying across her lap—her remembering how da Vinci had described it. She could touch it now, the horn, long, thick, fluted around the top. She had always thought it would be like a spike, but felt it filling out her hand as though the hollow of her palm needed it to join there as some strong secure limb.

She moved her hand down along it, the warmth flowing through it as it began to throb, and could imagine the mane like the hair she had just tousled, and the strange eyes, rolling lightly, smooth, oval, hard. She held them in the little-like forehead sack, their moving up over her hands, opening her, like curious tumblers, peering deep into her in the darkness, somehow guessing what was still there. She remembered once filling a balloon and placing marbles inside and letting them roll over her body at night in the attic with all the little rushes that would go through her, streaking along her skin magically all through the rubber, her suddenly having the desire she

[99]

would like these, so restless and shifting as they were, on her, rolling over her too. She touched the seam along their skin, like some scar, squeezing gently, holding them. Then she felt him moving in her lap and could remember the white little animal nuzzling there, the horn resting lightly, hard, and how that maiden might have sensed it too, taking it inside her lap to rub those moist oboe feelings all along from the inside, her bearing down to hold it there.

He began moving again, the knot in his shoulders seeming to let go. Then she felt him suddenly go deep within her. The summeriness, that meadow. Then the emptiness all around it, the swollenness spreading through her. She held her breath and could almost feel the ridges inside, like the smooth rings within a tree or those crinkly bevels on the inside of some flower vase when the image has not quite come through. She let her breathing move up along them, stretching and contracting, poised, shifting inside, not totally aware of the movement outside her and what she was doing.

Something was giving. Like a falling. Like her losing control. But somehow it was going backwards, pushing her up slightly, or her pulling it up, floating there with it, waiting, like something growing up all around her, a kind of longing she had never really noticed before, drawing up from deep within, like an ache, a pressure, completely unlike those alive surface sparkles she had had when he ran his fingers over her, along her, then his tongue.

It suddenly went deeper, all through her, as if falling higher, like a mammoth cave opening up just discovered, those rich soundings all there, then that longing wanting to come out, erecting in its own way, like all the swelling her nipples would feel, pushing out, hard, swollen, there, search-ing to be found, moving against him, filling all the space within his arms, around his loins, through his legs. He no longer crowding, but forming; not really there, but unfolding; all a part of that longing, her breath now seeming to enter

[100]

into it, helping it to open, uncrinkling from how long it had been packed away. And her feeling all the while, faraway on top of a mushroom, a tiny sleepy little "Oh yes . . . Oh yes . . ." smiling there for it to come out, as if blowing softly onto some beautiful flame that was about to appear, some tiny face, changing her, saying, "But that's who . . .," and her feeling all along, ". . . Oh yes . . . Oh yes. . . ."

HE HAD felt her body rising up against him, his head still by her breasts.

Then her face turning down, toward him, her throat by his, that close tight flutter, the pulse growing stronger, echoing in his ear, it coming up also under his hand like a spasm from deep within her, the throbbing suddenly rushing together, joining, the spasm bowing all through him from ear to hand.

He shrank back, twisting his face over her breasts. He pulled his hand away—it was crabbed and taut, reawakened—

[103]

and pushed it onto the smooth skin along her ribs. Then he
slid his head down, pressing his cheek against the flatness of
her stomach. It was like a sudden expanse of sky, away from
the warm curves and mounds of her breasts, opening, spreading out, higher, like a kind of broad anonymity that seemed
finer, smoother, cooler.

He heard her breathing come more quickly. He shifted his
weight.

There was a little sound, a whimper, that seemed a sudden
tiny swirl of water by pebbles. He held still, listening to her
breathing. His hand very hot.

It was like under the pier, after he had met his wife on the
beach. They were walking there, the tide out, and had gone
beyond the large tarred pilings, toward the back. There were
heavy concrete walls, green and hairy along the middle, with
black mussels bunched where the water had reached. They
passed behind them, away from anyone, and were by the
foundation under some old building at the end of the pier.
She started ahead of him, holding a finger up, as though about
to make a discovery; inside, the brick and stone were suddenly
different caverns and openings unfolding, one onto the other,
like multicolored stone vaults in the underground ruins of
some Roman amphitheater. Against one of the pillars were
two enormous chain links, just hanging there, rusty and
peeling in layers of thick reddish flakes. The air was cool,
damp. She looked around, as if viewing some new home, or
set, and looked at him, her blue eyes bright even in the
dimness under the pier. "I could *come* here." The smile was
there for the first time. Strange, open. He looked at her. There
were several flat jetty rocks embedded in the sand, gray, with
marble streaks through them, all smooth and rounded. She
went over to one of them.

He remembered the sound of the water, lapping softly
with the ebb tide, the pebbles and shells tinkling against each
other as the water swirled and zigzagged out; when it flowed

back, it spread out slowly, with a low open sound that seemed to echo from the angle of rock building up the back wall of their tiny chamber. He had reached out around her, supporting himself; the jetty rocks were neither warm nor cold, only there, and the curves were very hard, fitting close around the tautness of his body, impenetrable. He felt at ease, suspended. They lay there a long time after, his staring at the eyes, and that smile, that had never really changed. . . .

His hand glided down, opening wide in the little bony lake along the girl's waist, spreading to the coolness round the end of her hip, the little horn there. He rubbed his hand over it, feeling the smoothness entering his palm.

Then he found the tiny wave, the slight line where the elastic of the panties had been against her skin. He ran his fingertips along it, over it, the faint moist ribbing like the gill on the underside of a mushroom. He moved his hand below it lightly, finding the delicate down barely there, the cool fragile skin seeming as though it had never been exposed to anything, still soft, fresh, so that he could almost sense the tiny swirls within his own fingertips like snowflakes just lightly forming in the softness of that skin, then melting.

A little thread-like spring seemed to release; it was a fine line he could hardly feel unraveling beneath his fingers. He moved his hand down. He found her hair, long silky corn tassels, cool and moist, soft, winding around his fingers, growing in and out between them, his hand twining around gently. Then his fingers opened, tangling, letting themselves go, moving as though they were at the bottom of the sea, swaying, brushing slightly in different ways, as though some warm current were reaching down, riffling by, raising them up and down, carefree. It was like a quiet murmuring, making his hand forget. A numbness spreading through him.

Then suddenly it was there—a smile—breaking, opening, so different from the other when he had touched his wife's face. A lightness went through him.

[105]

His fingers had slipped down and over, touching the moistness, the little curve that parted. The silkiness guided him by and around, then over, circling his fingers down along the side. There was another little hollow, closeby, curly, twilled, mounding, then spreading his fingers out and over the smoothness of her legs, carrying his hand along and over again, toward the silkiness of that sudden smile in the darkness. Her legs trembled.

He became aware of how terribly dry he was, something there that had been sealed off for a very long time, deep inside, drained, parched. An ache that could not let out anymore, with all the relief it could bring, seeming somehow to have lost the way.

His body was sliding down. Flowing slowly over itself. His hands moving outside him, above him, circling gently. He could sense all the darkness still around his hands, his body, hollowing out as something he was backing into, more a pool created by his own movements. Different sensations breaking out like rashes over him, some sharp, distinct, others broad and dull. He remembered when he was on a netting before, he had slipped, his arm falling through the mesh or rope. A scratchy ring formed around the top by his shoulder. He withdrew his arm slowly, the scratchiness becoming sharper, more defined along his skin, until there were very fine pricklings of the rope's bristles on his fingertips. He had bent down for some reason and put his mouth on the rope, then stuck his tongue out: he no longer felt the bristles, there was just a stinging in his tongue, while the tip played around the barbs and hairy strands making up each bristle. It was odd then, his body becoming a harlequin of different kinds of sensitivity, more as some tactile lens moving closer, with pools of prickliness and softness all around him.

It was changing again, now over her, a nebulous dimension in his body, the lines and contours of sharpness spreading out before him as he slid down along her, ordering themselves in some new way. He seemed suddenly like an ancient African figurine, with thick lips, and broad uneven boundaries, enormous hands, and at the top, seeming to come from his head, a fine, moist filigree—sensing everything, everything flowing toward it, like a deep solitary eye in the darkness, the tip of his tongue.

He moved his hands down along her smoothness, a lightness at the base of his thumbs, the fleshy parts, sinking in, circling around, coming closer together, then spreading apart. The darkness slipped in cool through his arms, everything becoming more distinct, finer.

It was like a tiny earlobe. Warm, wet, sweet.

His tongue began to curl around it, holding the delicate flesh, moving back and forth, then sucking in. It seemed an incredibly moveable thing, barely there, that even his fingers could not sense in the same way; it made him feel the movement of his own tongue, darting, circling, curving, within the tininess of that space, as though all the possible paths and ways were contained in that one little seed, one appendage of motion, tripling up, around, crossing over, his tongue moving against it faster and more complexly than any word he could ever pronounce, like riddles and shibboleths of feeling.

It seemed to draw him in, projecting him back out, into something already there in the darkness, like a smooth wet handprint found somewhere that fills once touched as something different from just the ridges placed there, a whole other body playing out, sensed in the impress of one groove. A slow, heavy mass behind him, bunching up in the darkness, becoming lighter, changing, swelling, all that he would never have guessed at in the light, the more his tongue vibrated and twirled.

His fingers curled through the soft cool tassels, creating a sweet, moist halo around his mouth that seemed to seep into his skin, trying to relieve the unquenchable dryness so deep down, as though sucking up the fluids from around his tongue,

[107]

dispensing them here and there, unconsciously cleansing himself with some sacred balm reserved for the knight or battered warrior coming home to some maiden with his incurable wounds.

He moved his hands up slowly, stretching them out far from the movement of his tongue in a long languorous feeling as though more like a breathing inflating him, trying to reach into whatever was so empty. He had never really noticed his body before; how pliable, how sensitive it was. He had always thought of it in the most obvious way—a neat, symmetrical creature with two arms and legs, a trunk, a head. But that had all disappeared in the darkness as had the meaning of a day. And now, like that limp within him he had sensed earlier, so swampish and boggy, something else was beginning to come alive, to form, as yet indistinguishable, but trying to take shape in its own way, as with an old map filling out land lines of continents known from the name but which never could be recognized from the shape. An Atlantis. A body lost, submerged, deep along the bottom, all its older secrets still unknown.

His hands spread out over the tightness, the flatness of her stomach, then found the little knob, the distended navel with its nicks and ridges, like some small button under his finger. He stopped. He pressed it, feeling it give. *One, two.*

There was suddenly the strange sensation of another body lying over his, hovering, pressing down, becoming tighter. Then it was gone.

All that was left was the faintness of a shudder.

He reached out quickly to the sides, holding onto her waist. Her body, its softness, the curves smooth beneath his hand, for a moment only like some huge stopper, a body plug in the depth of that draft, whatever blindspot his fingers had somehow curled under in the darkness, finding a cool, hissy kind of nothingness lurking there all the while as when the taste of something breaks down, or when all the space leaks out from under some mask, deep, solitary, bottomless, everything else there just evaporating back out into it.

He kept clutching. Then managed to release his hands, pushing them down from their grip along the outside of her body; it was forming again, from that brief spell when it was no longer female or human, but only some rootless solidity in the midst of his despair. Her waist. The hips. The soft curve of her thighs.

He moved up, pushing his face against her breasts, then by her neck. He tried to imagine what they were doing, picturing that they were together, that it was dark, that she was warm, that he could sense the trembling all along her body, the shivering by his ribs. His arms closed over her back, his hands spreading along her skin, secure, safe, warm. Those curves guiding him back in away from that sudden hole in the darkness, the dizzy, out-of-breath, empty sensations sinking back through him.

He held close. Then felt the edge of her shoulder, small, rounded, seeming fragile and pliable beneath his hand. The bony little bump just up from the ridge.

He suddenly wondered how old she was. It was hard to place all the pieces and fragments of the time he had spent in darkness, their floating in, mixing themselves up with other things, leading one to the other. He was unable to form an image of her. He had never really seen her or even thought of her as having an age—just as someone there, that he had come to rely on. Without a name, without a face, only a presence. She seemed very young, the softness of her skin, the way she touched him, absorbing his movements in a way that an older woman would already have reacted to, pressing him into other things that the girl seemed not to be aware of. And yet her body was very full.

For the first time he really sensed the silence between them. The quietness. It was so rare that when he was in bed with other women he didn't hear the words, the need for talking, to say things to build the illusion, talking to make believe they were making love, as if the words could so quickly change the sex they really wanted into more than they could ever feel. He was aware of all that silence seeping through him now, calming him more than anything that could be said, or found out, making him only conscious of the exhaustion deep within him as though he were sinking quietly to the roots of seaweed somewhere, catching hold, letting the bubbles go up, then just rising, falling over her warmth.

She was pressing her cheek against him. Holding on. Her hand moving up against the hair on his chest, trembling. Then he felt her drawing little loops against him as if outlining ringlets of hair or making tiny, secret gestures, closing over something, hesitating. He became aware of her breathing, how faraway, held back it was.

He lay over her, covering her. She was a woman, a girl, made of all the things he had been told. Lacy, warm, tissuey. He remembered as a boy seeing his cousin naked behind the couch, hairless, her little vulva looking like the keyhole in the brass latch of his grandfather's old trunk, wondering what it would unlock. And the mystery staying, not knowing what to do.

He imagined the powerful fascination of seeing a full-grown vulva now, the hairiness, the opening, the swollen pinkness, how surprising that while all the other pin-up characteristics were curved, full and sensuous, what made a woman a woman, the very root of her had an appearance that was more compelling than beautiful, a mysterious, terribly faceless latch, that had turned him on so quickly as an adolescent, even if he only dreamed of it, before he knew how to open it, or what it could unlock in him.

He sighed.

It did no good.

He remembered how his wife would prime it. Each day with a new thing, her goodies, loving to make asides, little implications, "tickle words," she called them. Then her Kama Sutra monograms. She would sew different letters on his shirts, as positions for different days, FM or NS, or VT or KO, and although he would appear in class with them neatly embroidered on his pocket, no one ever questioned his apparent changes of identity, except Sandars. Then the PQ—as he did his work at home, her looking over his shoulder—with her relish at the hidden sexy thought of philosophy, the idea of $p \cap q$, the p's humping the q's, $\supset$ giving it to them, $\therefore$ one over the other, later sewing on a milky Q, a hole with a corkscrew in it, looking more like a $\mathcal{Q}$, calling it her academic box. And her joy one night of doodling M r s. on a piece of paper, and deciphering it as, *her legs wide apart, the little ball stand hanging over, twisting.* Then discovering as an actress that she could secretly play her role around a letter, and her practicing z all night, leering, $z, z. \ldots$

He held back, breathing deeply. There was a trembling all around him.

Then he felt the girl beginning to move against him. He began moving back over her. She was very tender. He had never realized his movements as he sensed them now coming back from over the girl, how held in, close, cramped, they were. It was very much like his handwriting, crabbed, his motion awkward and confused, restraining, like some person mortally afraid of showing that he can't spell and scribbling as if to pretend that everything is all right, proper, O.K.

He reached out again, finding the light curls of hair at the nape of her neck, then slowly brought his fingertips back over the rim of her ear, and down along her cheek, purposely dropping to her breast. He could smell the strong syrupy smell still on his beard, and remembered how he had touched her and how maybe that could close it over, the glimpse of that awful opening in the darkness, capping it as though it weren't there. Even larger than what had been in his hands.

Her fingertips were moving down along his body. Very

light, gentle, cool. Then the tingling. There was a tightness, a squeezing, a sudden gorging: he felt the erection.

He leaned forward, covering her, moving in. That tightness there, like a hundred tiny rings, each one squeezing, then popping as he entered, one after the other, until it became too wet to feel beyond the end.

Her breasts rising and falling unevenly, swelling.

Then his penis dissolving in the girl's warmth, the drowsy, lulling liquids flowing around him in the darkness, his moving harder, trying to keep it alive. It going slack, just like something in her, taken in, but with no frame—sealed off, lost there rather than opened, leaving him again on the outside as if he'd come to the edge of another world, some abyss out before him as he felt when he had first groped through the darkness.

The dryness was there, deep inside him, still parched.

He put his hands under her, bringing them up; he moved to the side, arching, the movement probing deeper, her legs curling over him, tightening, rocking.

He held back for a moment, closing his eyes in the darkness to shut everything else out, then twisted his hips hard against the girl. He could hear the sparks of hair as they rubbed and crackled. He concentrated on that, pressing harder, faster, feeling the rub up against that pubic circle, like a tactile zero, taking away, separating out, round and open, a pivot in the darkness from which everything else could take shape.

It made him think of the letters again and the ones he would never let his wife use or sew on him—the G and the X and the J—and the delight she would take in smuggling them in when she would put on her USO porno show, with columns of figures doing their own thing. Her pornoglyphics, as she called them. He remembered how they were all the Arabic ones, all the numerals, and was surprised at how much their motion revealed, so different from the little chicken's feet cuneiform on mud tablets that had come out of the Middle East long before. He wondered where the Arabs had got it from in the desert, and then felt the beauty of their words, snaking like the curves and softness of their women, some oasis of feeling in that dry world, ديوان بشار بن برد، ج ١ ص Like a whole alphabet coming out of a belly dance or harem, with the faint echoes of the numerals seeping into English as if some fertility dance that could still bring up the waters, a string of warm juicy numbers, dowsing: 26, 53, 69, 07, 98, 6201, 3625809.

They were flowing, moving in and out, the little number curves running through his mind to keep his feeling alive, growing, much the same way that he would once hold himself back, ironically, repeating a string of baseball scores to himself as an adolescent to keep it from coming too soon.

Her breath faster now. Then all his movements echoing. Their reverberating through him. Looping down. One up over the other, quickly like his handwriting, dropping, twisting across with a slant. Then the flurry that tucks it in all the more
. . . "𝜎" . . . "𝜎". . . .

THE VIBRATIONS went all through her. Bright, warm, like the cheshireness she had had.

And then she felt it growing, becoming larger. She held closer, knowing she was still falling somewhere on the inside, yet pressing, nuzzling her cheek harder—it all so different against his face, there, by her. Her seeming then to be balancing, slowing, something catching up, those tree rings, holding, coming together, one in the other, all inside her, all through her.

She rubbed back and forth against his beard. Then found his lips. The line, a soft pressure, the moment of recognition. Her lips becoming numbed, surprised, then tingling. She bit them, squeezing hard, letting them open slowly. She moved closer, touching his. It was like the white cloud of breath on those early mornings that came from her mouth, only now the cloud curling up inside her, wispy, warm, as though he had come closer, saying something to her.

She pressed back against him. His lips parted, moist. The tip of his tongue along the edge of her lips like a cherry pit waiting there after something sweet had flowed through her mouth. Then she felt the clasp of their bodies, the arms closing round, his holding her, like that handshake, squeezing, then swelling. Her just breathing deeply, something endless filling out in her.

He was there.

Then it was suddenly as if she were on a trapeze, the bar, the rod below her, in her, moving her back, swinging her far out into the darkness, to the very edges of herself, then returning with the cool rush of air pocketing out around her from the warmth of his body, the layers of herself, the rings, unwrapping, bursting, every time she came closer.

He could feel the tongue curling around his cheek, then the pulpiness of her breasts spreading out under him, the wetness of her skin as he moved, growing warm and cool, his body throwing itself into it, a rush of joy beginning, starting to soak through him, into him, out in the open, exulting, his mouth open, his tongue out to the side, his body as if scribbling, ... a steady, wide, even "O" ... then bringing down the loops ... slowly ... steady ... watching ... now, carefully, there ... a "G" ... oh God. ...

She dug her nails into his shoulders. Along the tight, thick muscles coming out from the hollows around his neck, holding into him, bearing down, his moving up, somehow as she held him her sensing his holding her and what it might be like

[116]

within the webbing of those muscles, within the cat's cradling of knots through his body.

Then she felt him twist harder, quickening to stay along her surface—pushing, pressing, thrusting. It moving higher. Like a Taurus. Ramming, butting, goring. She began cleaving, folding over, all around him, then joining together again, growing still larger. His energy, that hotness, meeting the billowing envelope of that longing, her enormous desire to absorb, to take in, to swallow.

Her seeming suddenly to lose a sense of how far she extended in the darkness but still knowing somehow how large it was as she moved, might be, could be, where it could reach, might reach. She had always felt that boundary, like a dizziness dreaming within her, as when she could imagine herself with some of the men she would read about when she was alone in the attic, her father in the studio. The size, the extent, the scope of that longing. She thought of Napoleon on those rocks in St. Helena, the enormous sadness that she would somehow be able to embrace, or in prison with Cervantes, or in exile with da Vinci, or in the South Seas with Gauguin, or hearing the drunken cry of Hoffmann at the end of his loves, lost, alone, with only the large breast of some muse able to bring him in closer, drawing off all those deep anguished feelings. And now here, hidden with him, groping in the darkness like a gorging caterpillar, in his great appetite for things, growing, swelling, ready to burst even beyond the limits of all she could remember about her father, moving now, spreading out, reaching into her, like one hard stone, piece, pit, dropped into the wetness inside, with its rings moving out, rippling, her own rings always slightly larger, tense, round, just barely keeping them within, while feeling his tightness pressing out against the limits of her own, her coming to be somehow at the very edges of whatever it was he was becoming, might become, would become, within her.

Then she swung back. Still balancing on the bar, the layers

peeling, wondering what would be left. All the blackness down along the inside of her legs, more as a little weight moving back and forth like the lead ball at the back of a doll's head, opening its eyes, making a cry. She could feel it rocking there, deep inside her, way at the bottom of her, and knew that if she had a soul, it must be there, balancing, all the layers of her body peeling back, opening, it more than ready to fly.

All the moistness. Spreading. Over his skin. Outside. Slipping over hers. Hearing all the sounds like the little suck holes under the pier, gurgling as the water flowed through them, spreading out along the sand. His hands groping over her as he moved, pushing into places he had never touched before, squeezing harder into the softness, the moistness, becoming hotter, absorbing.

Fucking . . . goddamn it. . . . . He was *fucking. . . . .* His remembering that hotness of those summers as an adolescent, feeling dry and parched without knowing why, and then those words, swearing, and all the mirage water they contained in their sounds, like musk melons, putting his mouth down on them, feeling the wetness, the coolness, the sweetness going into his lips, with all their onomatopoetic lapping. . . . *the sweet little fucking cunt, with its ass tight and open, screwing, sucking it up, the hard cock, balling, banging it away.*

He heard her breathing, her body expanding, the wet sounds, his penis tap-rooting down for all that was there. The succulent rhythms, their moving together, bodies pounding, like knocking heads together in those hot summer nights, fighting for the same space, as bump cars gleefully ramming into one another at the amusement parks, jolting, necks jamming back, shaking, all the pleasure opening like trapdoors down their young spines, and then the cool, hard, curving little trigger in the arcade, the miniature planes swooping down, red and blue and brown, with the thin hairline, pumping, flying out white in a straight line, shooting, then sometimes the hit, the blast of red and the *vroom* sound that blew together, seeming to go all through them, shaking, like a coming apart long before he knew what it meant, all hidden in that trigger and the plane that could be blotted out, and the girls they would take out after, riding in their saddles in some dark corner like pumping a trigger with their cocks, the idea of a red *vroom* light going on, some pleasure going to be there when it scored, their balls tilting, and the girls like some flashing thing to be turned on, shot into, so that all the tenseness of those hot summers could feel tight and cool around that special feeling like the triggers, tightening for real someday, with their tits and cunts as a training ground, like pulling rings out of the carousel for when they would make the big light go off and everyone know it, the world trembling all around, their bodies shaking, remembering the fun that were the arcades and funny houses then in all those bodies they used to bang away, never really having found their way in past the lights, lest they found something there soft and warm, alive, letting them feel things inside that would make all the triggers in the world seem too cold, too hard, too fast. . . .

She swung out. The little weight inside. Moving back and forth, rocking. That longing in her soul opening. Spreading its wings within her. Uncrinkling to flutter out from all that was left of her. Her sensing it there, as though there were no longer any other kind of weight inside. Swinging closer, waiting for that one moment. She felt his body coiling, uncoiling, holding, coming closer to her.

He took a deep breath, swallowing, his mouth opening . . . feeling that rub . . . feeling it filling him . . . feeling his blood throbbing. He pumped all the harder, his testicles slamming up against her, his temples aching. *Just fucking, fucking.* . . . Yet somehow slowing, holding back, his body beginning to swim, all his effort everywhere, pulling against him, though still moving.

She let go. *Yes.*

[119]

And then from nowhere that shudder was there again, like a cold wet kiss on the nape of his neck.

She only as if all the layers were suddenly slapping back, tearing against her, like a caress violently speeding up.

His just hearing the little lost cry—caught, tight, the quivering of a space around it, something else dropping out.

He had reached out. His fingers sinking in. It was soft and pliable.

The dampness of the skin. The hair. The slight poppling under him that began to throb, the swelling building up, becoming bladdery and thick.

He squeezed, pressing it harder. The windpipe caving.

The warmth coming round the trembling, then the shaking, and the muggy hot chill like a fever spreading through him. His own body seemed to be opening, as though something could slip into it. All his weight bearing back down on the man to shut it off. . . .

When he was alone and would jump out it was always more intense, faster, the training channeling it. Going for the throat with his knife, the jugular exposed, open. Being conscious only of not putting his left hand where they could get their mouth on it, keeping it high on the forehead and pulling back with the enormous strength liberated from that smell. Then finding whatever information was necessary and getting out.

It was later, always later, that he realized what he had done.

He might see the blood on his hands, steaming in the morning air, and then begin remembering what had happened so fast. The sensation of that warmth spurting over his hand, hearing that last sort of voiceless hiss, the fact that he went back and forth with the blade to be sure, then the strange sense of accomplishment. And what it looked like always coming last, if at all.

This one was different.

He had killed so many times he couldn't really remember anymore, but this one had seemed like the first. He had lost his knife somehow, crawling. There was that moment's hesitation by the bush when he discovered it was gone—then the figure moved—and he suddenly jumped out before he even knew what he was doing or would do.

His arm shot around the neck as though he still had the knife, pulling back tight, the wrist bone going flat into the throat. The man beginning to struggle, the shoulders humping back into his chest, then the head twisting around the crook in his arm, gasping, mouth going down, the hands coming back up and over.

He pulled back, slipping his hands down, clutching the throat from behind, straining to lift the weight off the ground onto his hip to stop any sound from coming out.

[122]

All the throbbing beneath his fingers, the muscles tightening, bracing, very much alive, pressing out against his hands, inflating. He pushed in harder, his fingers rippling against the fibery, squishy rings.

The man kicked into his shin, jamming it out. They were falling forward, twisting to the side, the sentry's body buckling up into his. Then they hit. The thud, all the breath giving, rushing out through his fingers, the dirt grinding, rubbing against his knuckles. He held on.

He should have let go. Dug into the eyes while chopping down on the neck with the edge of his right hand, or wrenched the head back, cracking the neck suddenly while he still had the chance. But his hand kept still closing around that throat, bearing down, his fingertips pinching in, feeling the space between them vibrate all the more, filling out within the grip, very solid, though it was only air.

There was a moment when everything tightened, a trembling all along the man's body, hard, unyielding. Then it all went slack, his suddenly penetrating. He was aware of how drenched he was, how he was shaking. Then realized that he was still on the other man's body—smelling that smell, though slightly different from his own—and quickly rolled off.

He could remember that no matter how special his unit's training had been, none of them had ever seen a dead body before coming to Vietnam. When they did, it was like an oddity lying there, its arms and legs out in some strange bent-over position. They would look at it, like dogs sniffing at something to be sure what it is, noting all the changes—the color, the smell—but never touching it. It didn't matter whether it had been someone known or not; it was a dead man, something beyond what they wanted to touch or talk about. It was too real. Later it was too common to be concerned about—another body. They would go on as if nothing had happened, though somehow still keeping their distance, as if from the first time. Everything seemed to be

[123]

done then at the end of something—the butt of a rifle, the blade of a knife, a bullet, a club—like running a stick along a fence, feeling what it's like out there.

Even off duty, while waiting for the next patrol, his men would avoid touching. Instead there was always the horseplay, the ramming and bumping and knocking around, to work off the steam, the edginess, yet never laying a hand directly anywhere, because of what that could always mean to other Americans. And him they never came near, for other reasons, shying away because of what they knew he could do, and how many times he had done it for them.

He thought of Pearse, the flushed face, cocked back, swaying, "So what the hell can you do with your hands?" and then remembered the touch of that sculpture, its smooth line, bringing him down to the catchy little gully inside the wood, and how Pearse had used the chain saw in the driftwood, cutting down into its knots until he had won. He could remember his own knife, how many times it had gone back and forth, the firmness around the handle, the slightly curved action as his wrist buckled out, and how the man he was killing was just filling in against his movement. ... It really wasn't a killing, anymore than a head bashed in under a rifle butt was, or a bullet through someone's heart, a grenade blowing up a body, or a chain saw cutting into wood. It was some kind of furious sealed-off violence, strong and spectacular out there, skillful, but never really coming close, where it could reach into, touch, what it was violating.

Then the other. He could still feel the strange knots in the Viet Cong's throat shifting beneath his fingers. How different from seeing something, then feeling how it goes together, moving. How smooth and tight the skin was, like a sheet of cork, yet how transparent that he could sense the ripples and pressures inside, rubbing close up against his fingers.

He had dug in savagely at first, wanting that edge, and then remembered backing off, surprised, relaxing slightly, his grip going loose, as the pressure, that presence, came. It was like a sudden catch—the deep swallowing, then the popping up—the knots becoming slack, then tightening, playing out in a vibrato against his fingers. A low guttural rhythm that entered into his hands, drawn out, wavery, like a sound heard under water. Then it became very distinctive, close, steadier, like the swirls of a person's thumbprint ... *one, two, three, one.* ... A timing, some rhythm, seeming to change the space, the reality of what was under him.

He pressed in harder, trying to shut off that windpipe, and yet found only an odd resistance there like a blindspot between his hands that he really couldn't reach into. He didn't know how. The fibers of the larynx seeming to have no part in it, being more like a wrapper around something else. He was aware of the strain in his arms, struggling, his hands swelling, firm, and yet somehow doing no more than massaging that throat, rubbing the skin up and down. He pushed harder, his fingers rippling, poppling against the windpipe as if pressing down different keys of some instrument. It was strange with no sound coming out, though he sensed things there, his wrists just rocking against the breath inside, against whatever it was he could not quite touch but kept moving back against him all the same.

He felt weak. There was a second that something seized within him, a kind of weightlessness, a shivering that seemed to be leaving, both cold and warm at the same time, as if his own body were opening, letting out a hotness that immediately cooled in some other draft there even before it had left him.

Then for the first time he had the shudder—like a throwing off of something trying to enter—and had the uncanny instinct that it would be impossible to kill what was there, that it was too unknown, unnerving, close up, and dark. It was easier to destroy or kill something he could get at, was aware of, that was known or routine, that he could cut

[125]

through with a knife, but what was coming out of that throat, pulsing in against him, seemed more to make him convulse, recoil, as though now he were caught there in some other rhythm, holding on, wanting the release more for his own sake, so as not to deal with what was so alien, so intense, or whatever else was coming out as something in himself that he could not understand.

He banged his face into the back of the Vietnamese's head, hitting his lips up hard against the skull, the pain spreading, the other things losing themselves. He was no longer sure what he was doing—just clutching, locked in, a dead calm, like something blacking out—though he knew they were both still struggling. He flashed on a statue he had seen in front of a building as a boy, one with a father and his sons wrapped up in snakes, all bound together, writhing. He didn't know what it was until after; at first it seemed only some tangled thing, a huge piece of sculpture moving back on itself, the way his arms and legs and fingers were all webbing together with the other man's, embracing, not quite sure where he was beginning or leaving off. He felt only all that fury going into it, merging, spreading, taking shape as something else his training had never dealt with. Very alive, very intimate. Human.

He began shaking. He squeezed the rings, the lump, thrusting it back in with all the strength he had left until it burst through. Then his fingers suddenly were lost, alone. He sensed the blip, the cry like a wet little sigh, just huddling against his palms, sticking there, as when he would cup his hands whenever it was cold, blowing into them, the warmth filling out against that hollow, hearing the strange sound that stayed there, like a clam shell, slowed down, echoing, very quiet. And that smell, all around him.

He had turned over, breathing deeply. Then crawled back into the jungle, groping over the dirt and vines and moist stalky leaves. He wanted to rub himself into it, drawing off all

[126]

its heat and odor. When he rested, he looked at his hands. There was no blood, nothing he could really see or remember from the morning as different. No sign of the killing. Only the blur of the face, no sounds except the scuffling, the fall, then that little cry, and the presence of something like it, there, in his hands, invisible, still pulsing.

He had tried then to recall what the dead body looked like, an image of its position, some picture, as a way of bottling it up, making it easier to forget. A Viet Cong, a gook sentry lying there, perhaps number 85. But all he could see were the elbows still angled out; he really wasn't sure of anything else about him, or who he was. Only the feeling in his hand. And then the thought after, that he might have enjoyed it. . . .

He wrenched loose. From her body. Those arms. Wanting the cold again. The numbness. The wetness inside expanding, filling in quickly, murky, as he moved, as if a hand brought out of the blanket late at night wiping a brow only to find something else there, thick, crinkly, soft, another surface like the outside of a body, a skin, yet more like entrails, suddenly sickening. Of what might still be underneath.

He remembered there was a clearing. The green leaves, the vines, the ground shrubs. She was there, the village woman, in the middle, next to the wicker basket, the food and other things he couldn't see piled in it. She lay down when she saw him, her eyes very black, her hair long and glistening, the skin creamy and tan. She stared at him, not speaking, then opened her blouse, the brownish skirt, the buttons popping, the breasts suddenly emerging, full, firm, as if just appearing from nowhere, standing out, swollen. He sensed that quiver. Her watching, those eyes so large and dark and glistening.

He could feel the erection, the long time that had gone by alone, lost in the jungle, and then suddenly that softness, waiting. She taking down her pants, scooting them down under her, the smoothness of her stomach, no underpants

[127]

beneath. As he had remembered at the other breeding camps they had discovered in the jungle where the Viet Cong kept women for their babies, always ready, waiting, as if new soldiers to be born from the thicket for a fight that would last forever.

He moved closer to her. His penis rubbing. Her lying back now. He could smell the air but only from the bristling at the back of his neck. Her skin seeming so creamy and tan, her eyes lárge, young, unafraid, waiting. Very beautiful, noble. Then he saw the bamboo, the little stalk at the side of the basket, almost invisible, the way fruits seemed to appear on trees and vines only to the guides who knew the jungle.

He could see what was in the basket, the supplies. She smiled. Her teeth parting, her nipples hard, the crinkly hair by her navel. Her hands were open, resting on their wrists by the ground. Then the slender stalk of bamboo that he could recognize by the tip. Her waiting, perched on her elbows, her pants off. His knowing what she would do. Moving down close by her, the smell, the warmth, so very deep, then that awful bursting inside as though suddenly drowning, his eyes closing, not to really touch her, the caution, the knot of hair in his hand, his knife out, the one quick stroke, then looking, her eyes never changing, strong, defiant, dark, the blood, the little sound escaping, that lightness of her neck forever in his hand. . . .

The ground suddenly dropping out. His memory writhing. More and more. Bringing back the quickness of that jump, without the knife, his fingers curling in, and the tightness of that throat like the defiance in those eyes, his joy of reaching into him, as if finding her, still strong, alive, the eyes dark and large and glistening, her breasts warm, waiting, mocking, making his body need to feel the extent of its manhood by pitting it, rubbing it up into the tautness he could feel in the other male, the poppling with his bare hands, as though in the same space as hers, lofty, apart, with the same tough fibers,

[128]

squeezing, untouchable, defiant, arousing him even more like some life-quenching savagery from out of all the emptiness that lay within him.

The joy. A keen fury. Himself twisting into it, twisting out of it, like a wild man, opening and closing at the same time. The fucking, the killing, both there, interlocking, exulting in it, enjoying it. Then a glimpse in the darkness of something monstrous.

He wrenched his body. He felt her, only her in the darkness, her breasts, the softness, the warmth of her loins under him, the blades pressing up. Her cheek was against his, in the curve by his neck; she was opening, as her hand had in the hollow of his arm when they were walking, her body seeming to change around him, wanting, flowing. Then the man, pushing down, his hands moving up around the back of his head, grasping. He felt her again. Then the moment from behind. The pulse of the throat, the smells, the sweetness, the syrupiness going into him from her skin, then the acridness, the odor, both coming closer, the rhythms beating, like those lights flashing red in the arcade, the skin sweating, always swollen, throbbing, beating, his body shaking, ramming back.

And then the horror. The lust, the fear, the death. Trying not to feel how you can fuck what you kill, kill what you fuck, the two ripping at each other in the same space, the feelings, the sweetness, mixing, unmixing, yet searing together, like some finger coming up hooking through two holes, as Othello must have found in that enormous jealousy, wanting and not wanting at the same time, killing and yet a kiss, but apart, coming back only in memory to destroy him; but now for him at the very same moment, like concussions of feeling in the confusion of darkness, held together by touching her, remembering the other, the grasp that can embrace or strangle, the closeness, the penetration, that can fill or pierce. The twin gift in being a man. The intimacy of both. Wanting to kill, wanting to make love.

[129]

He was shrivelling, his nails trying to hold into the skin. His mouth was forming. He felt the scream. Deep. Coming up. All the emptiness inside.

He rolled over. Over the breasts, away from the hands.

There was a scaliness, moving, scraping, pressing. A screeching, a grunt, a crashing within him that he didn't hear but was there vibrating all through him. Then rough plates pushing in.

His sensing what was waiting. Beyond even the pulse, that he couldn't kill or not kill. Some vast hole in the unknown that reached back through him like a primitive, hidden whirlpool of revulsion, opening, moving, contracting, carrying him off, needing him to fill it, the impotence like some monstrous suck-off of a vague other world. But something very real, waiting, there. That seemed to make all the prohibitions against touch some ancient throwback, as though all the language and visions and other bonds hoped to seal it off and thought they could take over all the contradictions of what that whole savage sense really held in store.

He had an erection. It was swollen, gorging, as if trying to plug it, the kind that comes from a noose around the neck, when the trapdoor lets go suddenly, the rope jerking, a wad of semen shooting out into the darkness.

He grabbed out desperately.

There was something. A twig, a branch, a throat.

His fists clenched.

Then a snap.

She heard it. The groan. The figure lumbering, rising, banging, crashing into walls.

Something fell, then the pounding, another thing turning over.

Then she saw the glow. She waited, thinking he had found the door. But it was still there, coming in flashes, somewhere in the darkness, a green, a yellow, as though he were trying to light matches.

[130]

She moved quickly.

He had crawled over the sandy flooring, then around the pile of fabrics and tubes, and squeezed by the edge. He found it. The wall with the sheet of cellophane swells or bulges like large blisters. He began stroking it. An eerie green flashed out, streaking along under his hand, cutting through the darkness like a St. Elmo's fire giving off its sudden light. He stroked faster, hearing the crackle of the plastic tissue, his eyes absorbing all the yellow and green ooze of the static electricity discharging. His face pressed up against the side of the sheet. His eyes bulging out. That foul, alien presence pushing up against whatever life was still there, thick, close, heavy.

He stroked the wall faster, making all the greenish light go out to it. Searching desperately in whatever was coming apart inside him now for anything else that could hold it off, offer a resistance from all the bits and images he could remember of his own background, his own culture, his family, his brother, his father's voice, his mother's face, the *blue eyes*, coming home, civilian life, sitting in the bathroom on the edge of the old tub with the clawed ball feet, his brother standing by the mirror, a white undershirt on, the electric razor rubbing across his face as he shaved, "Now that you're back, start thinking of what you want to do, things are a little different, but you know I'll help all I can," his making that frown and eye squint as he pulled his skin down tight meaning *it's O.K. if it's money for a while*, then in the restaurant, the little French café, all the large spoke-wheel lanterns with leather straps holding them, his sister-in-law sitting next to him, his mentioning about the beach, where he had gone when he first returned, to look at the ocean, and the woman he had seen lying there in the sun, the clear blue eyes, and the way some women have something special that does something for a man, even more than just being beautiful, making him feel other things, drawing him off, his brother overhearing, laughing, seeming stiff in his jacket and brocade shirt and wide tie, other

[131]

guests there, business associates, a lull in their conversation, "What's so special, maybe it's just being a good fuck," his brother saying, the others all laughing, his keeping quiet, very conscious of sitting there, stuck in a chair, being home, back with everyone, his brother still talking, the others holding wine glasses, pouring, passing cheese around, like moves in a game, someone commenting, apropos of the French café, with a maxim from La Rochefoucauld, that "afterall what is sex but the rubbing of two epiderms," his brother laughing again, "And that's the real rub," glowing, his eyes squinting, "But the best of his I remember"—just pointing his finger out into the air, heavy, thick, close, at no one in particular—"is, 'It's not enough that I succeed, my best friend must also fail,' " the others silent for a moment, then some laughing, he putting his arms over the back of his chair, pushing back, his arms growing heavier, more numb, becoming aware of the red light from the lanterns and the faces, the bottles of wine, the cuff links, the candles flickering like Christmas tree lights. . . .

"Every year, for godsakes, the same damn thing, it never fails, what is it with him?"

Those dark Etruscan eyes narrowed, upset, rushed with all the things happening, his father away at rehearsals, singing, then the parties, all the other opera people at their home, milling around, drinks in hand, all the excitement, the days growing still darker, shorter, sooner, no one noticing, the empty coldness there like a lump in his throat, it always time for his bed, a woman interceding for him once, the blonde singer his parents had talked about, her offering to tell him a story if he would say good night, and his asking, "Will you tell me the story of how you dyed your hair?" his voice very shrill, high, thin, nervous, "And if everything turns to gold when it dies?" his mother's lips, eyes, pinched, angry, the woman's face red, his body hot and cold, the darkness of the days like something coming to an end, then his father having to come into his room, just before Christmas, the strap hard, burning, strange, to calm him down, his crying himself to sleep to wake up settled, seeing all the lights again like leaves against the darkness, the day somehow different, the tree, the popcorn balls in colored cellophane, his mother in a long gown, all the family, friends, there, his father only pleased when he could perform in front of all the company to the question *who's the greatest singer in the world*, answering *number one my daddy, two Caruso, and three Beniamino Gi-gi*, everyone laughing, applauding, letting him stay up longer, making him forget how dark it really was. . . .

He stroked the wall harder, his tongue moving along the back of his mouth up to the roof, his throat throbbing, the sides of his upper gum ridges flat against the broad backing of his tongue. He started running his tongue over the bottom edge of his teeth, pressing the sharp ridges—*do re me fa so la ti do, do re me fa so la ti do*—hearing the scale play against the little sharps of his teeth, somehow holding him together in whatever was splitting, an awful urgency there, *do re me fa so la ti do do re me fa so la ti do*, his tongue stinging.

His father's voice running all through him.

Soft, sweet, mellow.

Arias, operas, the gift that had taken him out of the slums into concerts, his face preening in self-adoration as others listened, assuring him how much wider the audience such talent needed.

Blossoming into the golden sound, crooning.

Then nightclubs, hotels, trips back and forth across the

country, changing schools, conversations always the same, the deals, the hope, the poppling of champagne bottles just before things fell through.

His father starting to write his own songs in hopes of making a hit, posing romantically, the scarf, the jacket.

"Oh My Madonna."

"You Struck a New Beat in My Heart."

"You Can Sugar My Coffee, You Can Sugar My Tea, You Can Sugar Everything from A to Z But You Can't Sugar Love for Me."

The voice only changing, peaking, breaking, sandy, not being able to get back into opera, the *who they were* changing to the *who they knew* and *where they'd been*, changing to the *big break that would come*, moving back and forth, searching desperately for connections of a friend of a friend of a friend who knew someone who knew someone who knew someone who was someone, like all the rest of the "kikes, the lousy Jews," in radio, in film, in records.

Then his father's things growing worse, the face white, hardly talking, staying home day after day, his bringing food down to him, his mother complaining to whomever, "Believe me, you don't know what it's like having a depressed man in the basement!" his sister's face clear, crisp, sharp, "I'm not spending my life in a soup kitchen for any man!" the heels of her boots clicking against the pavement, "There are other options, and I'm going to get on with it!" looking down, the black asphalt, his brother's grin, "The way to make it is to find the cheapest way to service what people always need," his eyes narrow, slitting to the sides, "Parking lots. Where all cars go. The simplest help. The least overhead. There! How's that for a start?" the clever grin spreading wider, having bought the lot where he used to work, "The secret is, 'It always takes two, two names to seal a deal, no matter where or how you find the other one,'" his father coming up from the basement, shouting at all the neighbors, going about on the street where

[135]

they lived at night, his voice dry, hoarse, raspy, "I can't afford all of this! I'm broke! I'm broke! I can't afford all of this!" his mother red, moving again, the houses always worse, then his brother's head sticking up higher, from the sunroof in his limousine, visiting places where they used to live, "Eat your little hearts out, eat your hearts out!" his sister passing behind his brother's chair as his things got better, a family dinner on an Easter Eve, letting him know what someone had said of him, his just fuming, quiet, with beady eyes, his father mentioning something he had sung, on a parking lot somewhere under the company name, an advertising deal he had arranged on his own, with white tuxedo, sequined lapels, top hat, cane, "We're fortunate to have with us formerly from the New York opera, records, nightclubs, and screen . . .," then all the jingles, promoting, to a stand-up parking-lot audience, the little electric cords dropping down behind the jacket, his brother exploding, embarrassed for what it would seem, his father stuttering, sitting at the table, "I d-d-d-don't a-a-an-an-answer t-t-to an-an-an-anyone he-he-here . . .," the face deadly white, shaking, the voice very dry, raspy, "I-I-I-I a-a-a-am s-s-s-still t-t-t-the f-f-f-fatherr h-h-h-here! E-e-v-e-v-even if-f-f-f I-I-I do-do-do-do wo-wo-wo-work f-f-f-for y-y-y-you!" "Oh Jesus, shit, Christ, goddamn it to hell, Dad, you only answer to me so you don't have to to anyone else, don't you understand that, for christsakes, so *please* don't go out embarrassing me, not now, not now!" "I-I-I-I a-a-a-am s-s-s-still t-t-t-the f-f-f-fatherr h-h-h-here, I-I-I-I a-a-a-am s-s-s-still t-t-t-the f-f-f-fatherr he-he-he-here. E-v-e-v-even if-f-f-f I-I-I do-do-do-do wo-wo-wo-work f-f-f-for y-y-y-you!" ". . . oh shit, shit, shit . . . fuck it, Dad . . . will you listen!" slamming his hand down, others leaving the table.

All the sickness in the pit of his stomach, his fingers burning, pressing deeper, tighter, curling into the wall, blisters popping.

Her finally reaching him, seeing the faint blur of his body flickering, then hearing the sobbing.

She moved up closer.

He began banging the wall with his fist, hitting into her; then when he realized that she was there he suddenly curled an arm around her and held tight, his other hand still rubbing, letting that eerie green light flash out all the more, feeling the girl.

He closed his eyes, the memory of different ones coming back quickly from so long ago, open, dark, glistening, peering into his, their saying nothing, just lying there, so very young, and something so deep, warm, unafraid in her face before he took her in, making her seem all the prettier, strangely happy, as though sharing what had come between them, whatever might happen, however much it might hurt, if still together, his really not knowing what that all had meant then, only the lies he had said to get what he wanted.

"Do you love me? Do you love me?" Her voice hoarse, barely with enough breath. "It's only right if you love me." His answering yes, feeling nothing more than desperation, his voice very tight, clear, together, wanting only to smell the inside of whatever was there, wet, fleshy, feverish. Then later, when he would no longer look at her, aware even more of all the thirst that *yes* had left so deep, empty, inside him, as when the days grew shorter, darker.

Then those hands from behind the door, his giving them the bag with all the money, the girl going in, white, never seeing the doctor, if it was a doctor, only the hands, the woman, the nurse, whoever, the nauseous smell coming from inside, then the waiting, the imagining, the sweat growing hot and cold, seeping in all around him, everything quiet, nothing much in that office without the name on the door, all the old magazines, their ads with smiley beckoning pictures, nothing else much in there, only knickknacks, the toy bird up on a shelf, its red woolly beak dipping into a glass of water, then pulling back with its fat belly, pushing in and out, rocking, teetering down again, its throat up against the rim of the glass,

[137]

and his sitting there, trying so hard to wait, be cool, bigger than seventeen, doing what is right, thinking of all the things that could have happened if he hadn't, all he'd have to say, do, explain, provide, giving everything else up, changing his future, all he was supposed to do, becoming a doctor, yet the time making him feel smaller, more scared, the longer it got, making him wonder if he should have told, if he should still get someone, go in, tell, confess, help, wait, then his hands burning, rubbing hard along his pants, remembering the rubber breaking, the phone calls, the not knowing, the quinine, the alley meetings, getting the money, getting there late, the walls blank, only the hands at the door, the bird with its throat up on the rim, the time taking so awfully long, hoping, praying, then knocking, yelling, pounding, finally managing to break in the door, no one else there then, not even an office, only the girl on the table, her skin all waxy, the way those little candy bottles look when all the liquid is drained, the color of a condom left behind, her legs wide apart, all the blood on the table, on the floor.

Then his going into the army, with all the flares, the bombs, the red traces, phospher trails zigzagging, giving distance, shutting it off, burning it all away, groping out, going through all the motions slowly, again and again, until anything anymore like a response had changed to reactions, clear, tight, sharp, the smells just sour, acrid, crawling along the ground like some obstacle course for whatever had to be done, simpler than anything that had to do with girls, or feelings, and yet still at times weighted down as though all the tangles of the jungle had filled in, closing over, like those little crystals one has as a kid that grow up in some magic garden solution, the different shapes and twists and colors connecting up in funny ways, jelling, some of the crystals always at the bottom left doing nothing, then just lying there, deep in some foreign land, at night, no stars out, the lights suddenly bursting, the rumbles faraway, the darkness again, then the silence, all alone, remembering an awful homesickness going through him, of family, friends, those dark eyes, yet knowing only too well what there was to come back to, the few seconds it would take to realize why one had left in the first place, but the sensation there like wanting the softness of an arm within his, not knowing where anyone was going, just going, together, more a homing sickness in some darkness, sensing there was or should be a somewhere, some special anywhere, that was home. . . .

His brother sitting there, after dinner, behind some old carved baronial desk he had bought, thinking, his face jowly, intent, very much like the time he sat there looking at him sadly, saying very quietly, "I'm the frog, you are the prince. But there's no telling what I can turn into, really," his face squinching up, "And they'll kiss it then, they'll all kiss it."

His brother looked up. "There's something I have to do that I don't really want to."

"Then why do it?"

"The opportunity's too great."

Pushing the cleaner into his pipe, the brown color on the short white bristles going back and forth inside.

"When everything is equal, only cunning tips the scale. And if you're not winning, you're being outplayed.'

His eyes lowered.

"You never know where the hand you shake has been, but then living well is the best revenge. In the end, a man judges himself."

"After a certain point, in the end a man judges himself."

His looking up.

"What the hell is that supposed to mean? What I said was simple. In the end, a man judges himself."

"There are standards, things to be learned before you reach the point where in the end you can judge yourself. You're not alone. There are others."

"Holy shit, all I said was a fucking simple thing. 'In the

[139]

end, a man judges himself!' That's it. There's all there is to it. There's no point. Anybody, everybody, a rock, a kid, a goat, in the end judges himself. That's it. What do you have to do, watch every fucking word with you! Is that it?"

His face glowering.

"You annoy me. Do you know that?"

"I was only trying to be of help."

"Help. You've got that damn sneer on your face, patronizing, patronizing me, that goddamn half-turned-up smile like you know so fucking much. In the end, a man judges himself. *Period.* That's what I said, that's what it is."

His getting up.

"You know, damn you, I've been to college too, I've got mental riches too, otherwise would I have what I do, or got where I've got?"

His pointing to all the trophies, business, political awards he had set up all over his living room.

"You're a fucking selfish bastard. Just because you teach philosophy now, you suddenly know, you're better, you're on a different level? So you have a philosophy, I have a philosophy, it's that fucking simple, nothing special, just an opinion, yours, mine."

His arms swinging out, round-elbowed, his hand jabbing down, as if about to terminate one of his audiences.

"Why, is philosophy suddenly in the yellow pages?"

"No, why, are you?"

"I? I'm in more than you think."

Bringing his hands back in, cupping them to his breasts.

"Have you ever seen yourself recently, really seen yourself, what you look like, the way you preach, I'd love to hold a mirror to your face, you think you're so much better than the rest of us, and I always thought you were an angel, sweet, naive, trusting people, I admired you for that, I thought it was nice, and what I could of done if I had half of what you started with, all your looks, but you're a fucking snob, you're

[140]

posing, you're a phoney, a fucking supercilious posing fucking phoney, afraid like all the rest of us."

"Of what?"

"Of being found out, you high and mighty prick, pretending to be up there so fucking smart, and when I, I, paid for all that fucking philosophy, afraid to admit you're like the rest of us, down there, man, down there, you supercilious prick!"

"I don't claim to know anything."

"But you act like it, it shows in your face, like you're always judging, like we have to watch our words. But there are no angels, there are no little princesses, it's all pornography, we're all pornography, everything, everyone, love, truth, heaven, this country, it's all pornography, we're all in the shit, and you think just because you had to go through all that shit over there that you're exempt now, that you were a victim of something that gives you a special privilege, letting you lord it over us, well you think I haven't been through shit, right here, building into something, you think it's just been given to me, something I was born with, that I didn't have to do things I didn't like to, to get where I am, *hah*, but that's all behind me, I don't dwell on it like something's due me, I just keep on building, and the only law there is is that one hand washes the other, but you somehow think you're above the law."

"No."

"Yes you do."

"There are other laws."

"Name one, you fuck, that can't be bought."

"There's a truth."

"There you go again, you high and mighty bastard! Listen, you're my brother. I wouldn't shit ya, I'm concerned for you, your welfare, others would have written you off long ago, I never have, I try to understand, but because of that pose you never open up, with what's inside, what makes you tick, with anything I can get hold of, you're a rough guy to get close to."

"No, not really. It's very easy to. You just have to have

[141]

something to get close with. But I guess you'd know more about that than I would."

"You fuck, you lousy good for nothing fuck, see you'd talk ten thousand trees around me before you'd ever admit anything, that you're afraid too, in the shit too, or even come to me, with that fucking pride of yours, never stooping to ask for anything."

"You haven't anything I want."

"Oh really? No, but your women are always asking for you."

"Who?"

"Never mind. I can name names."

"Who?"

"Your *mother*, your *sister*."

"And?"

"Your own *wife*, damn you."

"Asking for what?"

"That you be helped."

"But there's nothing wrong."

"You think so, but they're putting it on my back. They come to me for that. Don't you realize you stupid son of a bitch that I'm the head of the family, that I'm the one they all come to, that I'm the one they all work for, that I'm the one responsible for everything you've done, for all your careers, how do you think your wife got that part, from Feindahl, hell I've got his stock, and I'm sick of it, I'm sick of all of you, always wanting something, using me, and always their concern for you because of what you've been through, harassing me, others embarrassing me in public and just when I'm beginning my political career, no one making things easier for me, worrying about how things look for me, for what I have to do, what I have to risk, well shit you're a fucking thorn in my side with that fucking face of yours patronizing me, judging me, I don't need you to tell me anything, I don't need

[142]

anyone, you're all pains in the ass, I'm through with the lot of you, fuck, in this country you can divorce a wife but not a brother, a family, well goddamn it, I divorce thee, I divorce thee, I divorce thee!"

His banging on the desk, knocking over his awards.

"Do you know that with the money I have I could buy a small country? Do you know who I know? That while you were in Vietnam I had more than you can imagine staked over there, with more people than you can ever imagine, where did you think all that building, all that asphalt, all the construction came from, and with who I had to deal? I know what people want! And then you have the nerve to insult me with what you think, calling me on a point I didn't get right like I was some kind of fucking student of yours. Have you ever heard yourself, listened to yourself, with all that bullshit you come up with, that craziness, that worries everyone. 'It's dark.' Alright. 'When the lights are out it's dark.' That sounds like you. No, it's dark, you dumb fuck, that's all. Like in the end, one judges oneself. So in the end, it is dark. That's it. Clear, simple, period! In the end, I might as well be the professor."

"According to La Rochefoucauld, 'In the end, prostitutes always seek respectability.' "

"Did he say that?"

"No, but he might as well have."

"You cock-sucking shit!"

Stepping up to him.

His angling sideways around the desk.

"Oh, no, I'm not getting into that. I'm not going to get into that with you. You're just jealous, you phoney, why don't you admit it, you just haven't got it, you haven't got what I've got."

"The only thing you've got that I'm jealous of is a child."

"Then why don't you have one, you fuck!"

"That's my business."

"I'll bet it is. You can't get off your high horse for it, huh? Get down there with the rest of us pornographs and just fuck!"

"Listen, I'll confess something to you."

"Oh? Yes?"

"Are you a homosexual?"

"No"—his eyes suddenly brightened, aglow—"Ah *hah*, so that's it! I always knew there was something with you. . . . No"—a superior look—"I'm not that way. Is that what you are?"

"No. But I'm not your way either."

"Oh, you miserably fucking ungrateful bastard, don't you tell me that, because I'll tell you, you son of a bitch . . ."

His face inflamed, shaking.

". . . I'll tell you who I am, you fucking phoney, with all my power that makes you afraid to go into a grocery store and sign a check without your name being recognized, reminding you."

"Who told you that?"

"You know. You know. Reminding you . . ."

His finger jabbing.

". . . You know what I mean. You know, you know, you bastard. And you're afraid to own up to it, admit it, that you haven't got it, with all the promise you were supposed to have!"

"Reminding me of what?"

"That you're the failure, and I'm the success!"

His banging on the desk.

The growling.

The explosion.

The rage.

The sounds poppling from the throat. . . .

His wife's voice peaking.

The smell of alcohol, cigarette smoke.

The hotness at the door.

[144]

The tightness of the blindfold.

"Well, I guess I shouldn't have expected more from a philosopher. It just does wonders for a woman. All that platonic love. I'll bet Plato couldn't get his up either! And whenever you decide to drop in again, remember all I need is just a good fuck! And if you're not going to give it to me somebody else will, and if I should happen to get pregnant it won't be my fault. We'll always say it's yours—won't we? I'll just say you came back one day 'cause you just couldn't take it without me anymore, whatever the fuck it is you're doing, and we'll just hope he has your eyes, you ungiving bastard, because he's going to have your family's name! Maybe in more ways than one!"

The smoke in his face.

He opened his mouth.

The door slamming.

His breathing heavily.

Holding onto the door for something real, tight, clear, so as not to rip off the blindfold, knowing suddenly.

"Oh God, you fucks, you lousy fucks!"

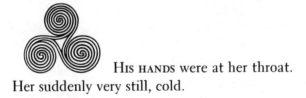 His HANDS were at her throat.
Her suddenly very still, cold.

His jaw shaking.
The muscles pulling in his shoulders.
A chill going up and down his back.
The poppling coming around his hands.

His fingers kept pressing in.
Her moving her head quickly then from side to side.

[147]

Sliding up her hands, bringing them down over the fleshy parts of his thumbs.

Hot, stifling.

Holding her breath longer.

Trying to find some part of her body that would let her escape.

Thinking only of the little wooden doll, of Sid, that hotness, the lunging, something to take her higher.

He pressed in harder.

Her swallowing deeper.

Becoming fainter, weak, dizzier.

Her body hot, muggy, closing round, pressing.

A stream of air all along the tip of her tongue.

Its coming out.

The tiny pulse.

That rhythm.

"Oh you fucks, you fucks, you lousy fucks!"

There was a rush of coldness.

Her throat curving back.

She bore down, her skin drenched, clutching her fingers into his arms.

Everything catching in her throat, her straining against it, barely able to breathe, like the ether she had read about the gods and the view from Olympus that had surprised her so, her father wanting to go there, that air so scarce, the snow dry and powdery, everything silent, exerting herself to keep going on, following him wherever he went, no matter what he did, never believing he would hurt her, but her body changing, her breath lighter, her lungs heavier, then seeing the high scoop of the main peak that everyone took for the whole of Olympus from the distance, the broad, curved face of it close-up like an amphitheater as if she were moving across a huge stage, its scooping her up, throwing her back, making even the tiniest things she did seem more important, so unlike what she had later felt in church, siphoning her off, giving nothing back, and the damp little nunnery cells, her cheeks tingling there, burning, blushing in the cold air.

She had moved closer to the edge. The sky so different from what she had remembered later when she had stopped believing in God, giving it all up, breathing more, faster, harder, even if she would die, no longer wishing for some reward to change her, but only to disbelieve in Him, not wanting Him, letting Him look away, only to love Him more, like her father, her not minding, however damned she might be, or what He might do, her love now her own, that she could risk it all as proof of her, what even He had never done, testing His strength in not being alone, yet still needing a son to cry *Why hast thou forsaken me?* simply to please Him more, before He knew that He too might have a daughter who would never cry out, wherever He might hide, from all the love she could hold within, her body shaking with her choice, trembling, colder, in all the air that rushed away from His silence.

But the sky in Greece so open, vast, filled, after the climb to the Throne of Zeus, the bright blue swallowing the snow in front of her, nothing left, all the heavens seeming to surround her, her head floating, her breath in the pure air dreamy like the first time she had wine, as giddy as the quivering in her glass, then her head lowering, looking down. All of Thessaly was there. Swollen green meadows, smooth, rounded, spread out at her feet. There was a richness, a softness, as far as she could see, the fields growing, expanding, curving with smaller mountains humping over, not of rock, but of a smooth dark earth molded as breasts. She turned away, as if all the smells, garlicky, sweet, nauseous, of the earth were rising, but faraway

[149]

in the glinting blue seas other risings of foam-ringed earth met her gaze no matter where she looked, like stars that connected up in the sky, her eyes coming back down, forced always to fall back on the soft green lushness below, wondering why God was always so alone when Zeus had so much to look down on, a lump in her throat, tighter, her breasts suddenly heaving, realizing that down deep it was a woman's world, and that she was a woman now, full, fertile, open, waiting, that no one could ever take away, as once she had wanted God to, that could only be shared unlike the damp, sterile air He gave from all that was so alone, if she could only breathe in that other space, all the smells, that were so thick, penetrating, deep, all around them. . . .

Her hands shot up quickly over his back.
Their nipples touching.
His shoulder blades rounded like small mountains.
Stretching out over her, holding there.
That smell of ether, strong, pungent, coming from between his legs.
His palms by her throat, all the fullness within her pushing back out, swinging her hips up.

She pressed her lips tight together, her breath crisp and sharp along her nostrils, a bitter taste at the back of her mouth, holding more closely to him, yet her hands somehow outside of her, like the rubber wall again, tight, cold, impenetrable, except that it was as though her hands were on the other side in the darkness by his arms, in his arms, even the warmth of her breasts from all the flutter of her heart out there with him, beyond her, no matter what he might do.
She rocked her face against the side of his arm, the way she had remembered once in the room against his hand, letting her feel with him what she had never felt before, all so total, hurting because of him, yet there because of him, living

[150]

because of him, feeling because of him, her lungs catching, quivering, her skin drenching again, finding herself teetering on the edge of some huge abyss, either way, the choice there, the doubt, the hope. . . .

A breeze went through the hollows of their skin, then was hot again.

His hands closing and unclosing.

His fingers pressing in at the back of her neck, palms against her throat.

His thumbs sliding back and forth across, pushing down.

Her boundaries shifting.

The space opening up all the more from around them.

Something happening, very fine, growing through the center of her, tugging up from her loins, as if breathing from within, a vine, a blade of grass, a thread wanting to go out as some other part of herself as with that first flush of warmth in becoming a woman, her seeming to understand the space her mother might have lived in, another side, and how that happened, and why the paintings of her father never looked like her, no matter how much he tried.

She kept turning her head from side to side against his palms, her head rotating, all her bones shifting, the lightness releasing into a ringing all around her, not knowing where it could go.

The rest of her body billowing, moving apart through her like skin ready to slough, bright, warm, tight, as the mermaid who wished for legs with all their pain, the lines down the center as though teeth ready to come out, to touch, to leap, to dance, on some new ground, yet staying there, the ground rising.

Seeming a little wobbly. All along her stomach. Not knowing what to expect, what to feel. As with wearing high heel shoes for the first time, trying to balance. Holding back, yet feelings coming here, there, grazing up against her skin.

All in the way she had imagined her mother's body could grow lighter, everything pointing away from the ground, keeping a dancer still higher in the air, all the musicians secretly helping to raise her there, the oboeist hunching up his shoulders, his throat blowing out, the flautist lifting his eyebrows, the timpanist in some last thunder roll letting the sticks rest higher in the air, all the violinists sweeping up their bows, stroking across her, fingers curling, vibrating along that one spot where the music could come.

It all pushing her higher into some other forgotten envelope of herself, still there, alive, waiting, an odd amnesia along it, as though all one's feeling kept going on, never lost.

The two men there waiting, only the swish of that long hair, never coming into her room anymore, the hand always on the wrist, fingers around it, pinching, not warm, and the voice suddenly high, peaking, as if speaking on point, all the arguments, the birthday cake, the silence, the kitchen knife suddenly slicing across, taking off the top, not blowing it out, all the spongy holes left inside, moist, white, cool, parts of candles still there, nubby, like roots of baby teeth left behind, never falling.

"After having you I even had to learn to walk again. I was an artist. All he wanted."

The two men there, waiting, her father looking at the paintings on the wall, the droplets on the floor circling all around, like the wavy pattern at the hem of one of her dresses, her mother standing there, having left a trail over the floor, urinating like one great mama doll, then not moving anymore, just dropping down, wearing her cranberry dress, her legs to the side, her wrists crossed, the two men there, a cot brought in, making her lie down, her never saying anything more, nor moving, her father looking at the wall, the droplet on his face, like all the droplets on the floor, then the siren echoing faraway, making no more sense at all. . . .

[152]

She suddenly bit into his skin, holding it tight between her teeth.

Breathing in, over, sucking the air in around that fold of flesh in her mouth.

A strong smell with it.

Biting harder, hotter.

The coolness coming after making a slight whistling sound against his hair.

Trembling.

Sliding her hands along the moistness of his arms, just up by the shoulders, like sanctuary, below where the vaccination mark is, the warm bulge of those top muscles, just over the incline of her grasp, her fingers spreading slightly apart, as though they belonged, full, snug, no matter what else they felt.

Then her fingernails pressed tighter into his muscles, the tip of her nose against his chest, her heart moving out into the surface all around her, beating quickly in a different time, not breaking, feeling cleansed, fresh, virginal, pure, beautiful, untouched afterall as a woman, there nowhere for Sid ever to have entered her, whatever he had done, or why, her never having dreamt of him, her still in the long-necked urn she had spun into from dreams of her mother, closing over, only that one spot left at the very top, its long neck open, waiting, she still inside where she had dreamed only of him and all the shadows she had seen in him in the room, her moving faster against him, her wanting him to feel that one spot where she had dreamed of him, where only he could enter if only he could find it, her body swelling all the more now to the depth of a beautiful new moment all in its own time, tight within her.

It was as if she had suddenly remembered. Very clearly. The forms of those bodies. Meeting so perfectly. As no one had ever told her.

That statue of David, his right hand down strong along his side, his hip slightly out, the other arm curled up to his shoulder, his face turned to the side.

Then the painting she had seen. The Venus of Botticelli. The body rising from a shell, the left arm down gently along the curve of her waist, her leaning, the other arm folded up over her breasts, her head turned down to the side, her hair blowing.

Those opposite sides so exact. Fitting so well. So beautifully in some secret moment of an embrace. As if made to come together. From wherever they were, apart.

A chill went through her. Different, electric, tingling, of how they belonged.

She squeezed her fingers. Bringing them up to the very edges of his shoulder. Like David's. His arm, hers, matching, hands cupping. Moving her legs closer to his.

"Oh hold me, hold me, please just hold me!"

He let go of her.

His eyes wide open. Blinking.

Running his hand along the surface again, letting that eerie green light come from the wall to see who it was, wanting something specific, individual, fitting back into real things, distancing himself as could the world that he knew was out there beyond the darkness, with faces, cars on streets, buses, dogs, people with eyeglasses, office buildings, windows, an outside, a background, something he could see that would re-contain, bracket all that was coming loose within him.

But his hand was frozen. Her fingers clutching into it, pressing back hard, her breathing clear, strong, the tightness of her muscles straining against his, a moist coldness all along her body.

Then her arms moved out, one catching under his neck, her weight going back, exploding, his body yanking up in the enormity of her strength, spinning over, turning, moving down along a flush of hotness breaking out all over her skin.

He was falling onto, into her, her energy holding him in closer to her, one arm curling around, another powerful arm, then a leg, her body twisting up in the same momentum, pushing, rolling, turning them away from all that was at that wall.

There was a quick drop.

Her holding still closer, his stomach going up all the more.

Then a thud. A bang.

A caving inside him.

An enormous blast of heat.

Her weight pressing in deeper.

He reached out, flailing for anything that could be taken hold of, touch ground with, enabling him to pull away from her.

But she kept spinning, however small her body, keeping him off balance wherever they were, her movement toppling him over, up and down, around, her hands grabbing hold of his shoulder, her fingers clenching in under the girth of his collarbone, wrenching in near yet pushing away at the same time, her legs curling under him, there no place outside he could find in the darkness where he could get away from all the rush, the heat, the tangle of her energy, pressing into him, coming up under him, over him, closer to him.

Then they hit up against something, or bumped, or crashed, or dropped again, or her abruptly stopping to spin, holding back tighter, everything else flying out still further within him.

She just lay there, releasing her grip.

[156]

He waited. The dizziness like in those rides in the amusement park where the bottom drops out. Then the pause. Just hearing her breathing. The slight sniffle. Faraway. The almost voiceless sigh.

He touched the lumpiness of the flooring inclining up around them.

She was angled over him, her body burning.

He struggled to sit up, pulling out from under her yet holding onto her for support, suddenly realizing all the uselessness of how his muscles could coil or crouch, what the training had instilled, all the self-sufficiency as a man, there no moment, no target, nothing he could spot, as though action wasn't really possible in the darkness, only reactions, only responses.

She did nothing.

He glided his hand along the smoothness of skin as he moved up, the long line that dipped in softly by her waist. He pushed his hand down and found the underside of her thigh, the muscles taut, hard, then moved his hand back, his palm rubbing over the hair there, the joining between her legs like some smooth gully taking his hand down, across, bevelling; he moved it up quickly along the other side, then back again, over her hip, her buttocks, returning over the silky hair just as that little mound began to rise up from across her loins.

She began shaking.

He tried to imagine only the objects in those glass cases at amusement parks, the pin-ups, matches with the dirty pictures on the back, the boobs, or the stockings, or garters, or zippers down the back of a blouse, a shoulder turned, and the kewpie dolls and rubber snakes and ashtrays and keychains with the plastic pressed spiders that were always somewhere in a dirty glass case to be redeemed for the endless tickets of some skiball game and meant so much to hold after a whole night trying to reach their score, the nude plaster-of-paris figurines, the big breasts with the red painted nipples, and the one of the little boy, half crouched, always peeing over the edge of

[157]

some cliff, all the shapes of those cheap little things that could be won, felt up, standing out all the more like good hot-ass things in those magazines and dirty comics with cunts straddling legs and pop-eyed breasts hanging over, the clear curvy bodies grinning, squishy, head to toe, coming on, ready only as so many soft warm things to be pinned down, stuck into, had, clear, simple, there.

His hand grasped into her harder, his finger curling under, breaking through, struggling to maintain control of that little mound, that joining between her legs, then it started squeezing, buckling over, both her legs suddenly moving closer together, one slipping over the other, catching, folding his hand, clamping it deeper between them as she twisted down to the side.

His other hand shot down to grab hold of her but immediately sensed all the tightness and power of the grip of those legs tensing across with no way in, locking in his other hand with a strength stronger and harder than any he had ever found struggling against another man's arms, the image of all that femaleness flashing through his mind, how supposedly long and slender and graceful the build and yet in reality like some invulnerable vise, making him remember when he was in school in a class with only the little girls allowed to do those beautiful gymnastic flips and turns around the bars, from higher to lower, then realizing why with all the exposed weakness between his own legs ready to slam up into one of the bars, recalling all the more those party nutcrackers his parents only brought out for company, the curved female legs with the hinged hole at the top and the quick giving-sounds of those tough shells surrounded, cracking, the women always laughing, smiling.

His body tightened.

He reached out, her body tilting up, not knowing where he thought it would be, or would go, his fingers grazing against the small silky crevice that traced out from her back into the warmth and fullness of her buttocks, his hand hovering there for a second, very open, exposed, confused, sending back a different sense of himself as it formed over her, not really knowing what she was doing.

He tried to find her ankles. Attempting to spread them wide. Imagining them joined together. The hair, the strength, the crack in the center. Pearse cutting down into the knots of a stump. The cunt without a cock, the loss, the lack of a penis. Nothing there clear and sharp and hard. That can give direction, that can point, focus, be gone into with, like the sound of a bat hitting a ball, a cause, an effect, making another thing go, get away, fly off, wham, slam, smack.

He quickly slid his hand down. Then that crack seeming like a fold. Smiling slyly. Proudly. A turning in that keeps turning out. Like those Chinese fortune cookies with that dough just bent over, folding in, the lips barely apart more as a little cunt holding a future inside, some piece of paper all curled, the way his mother would make up her mind writing her thoughts down on different slips of paper, curling them up, putting them in the steamer, with whatever one opened first what would be, all the others still curled or half opened or lying around, wet, soggy. His touching it now, wet, soft, warm.

The girl twisted to the side. Her body moving against the tremors in his.

He caught his breath.

Then she slipped out, her arms and legs mirroring his, staying close to him as though his whole body were doubling, playing back on itself, not knowing what it really was.

He was under her, below her.

He heard the girl's breath. Long, deep.

Her hand was at his forehead, the tips of her fingers along the creases, discovering the furrows there, caressing, cool, wiping back the moisture. Making him only remember that other hand. The tousling of his hair on top of his head, or over his forehead by his eyebrows. Or the light fingering there on his shoulder when someone was leaving, his standing on the porch, fitting just under her arm, holding him in closer whenever the company left, still talking to them, about whatever, then begin to caress him, bringing him up all the more under her, holding him affectionately for a second as the people left, letting him feel that closeness, her hands, their warmth, before they went back into the house, and then the awful, empty distance it somehow always left behind within him, never coming closer, as if those feelings were to remain forever on the verge of something faraway, not quite clear, out there.

A shiver passing through him. Bringing out very dimly that first time lying back. In the little hotel room. Everything dark. Her afraid of being seen naked, he had guessed. Having met the woman on the street, her walking across the hotel to the café, only to look in the window. He came out to talk with her on a dare from his friends, then was surprised by the elegance of her speech. She was considerably older than he, he still in his early teens.

When they went back to her room, she sat up on a barstool in front of a kitchenette counter, drinking from a water glass full of gin. She lit a cigarette, her hands very long and slender; she said she had studied piano at the conservatory, when he asked, and then asked about him, just staring at him, no matter what he said, as if not really caring. Then she got up and came over to him and said, "Please, let me," and began undressing him, with a quiet, wistful tone in her breathing. His smelling all the alcohol coming back over him.

"I once played Bach and Mozart in Europe. Now I celebrate you. But that doesn't mean anything to you, does it?" He didn't answer, only watched a little more carefully, a little colder, wary. Then she went back to the counter for another drink, picked up her cigarette and dialed on the phone, switching off the lights. He could barely see her undressing from the glow of the bathroom light, the telephone receiver still pressed with her shoulder to her ear. His almost thinking he should leave.

She began laughing suddenly. High, strange. Like nothing

he had heard before. "Hello. . . . Hello yourself, you son of a bitch! Never mind where. Do you know who I have with me? Do you? A young god. An Adonis. Do you hear that? A god. A young god. How does that seem to you?" She turned abruptly, holding out the phone. "Say hello." He said hello; he heard the older man's voice on the other side, very tired, drawn. She pulled the phone away. "So there, you cock-sucking, son-of-a-bitch bastard! Now see if I care what you think." She hung up.

She turned out the bathroom light, then came quickly into the bed, the heat and smell of her body radiating as if triumphant, gloating. She covered him with the softness of her skin in the darkness, crying out weirdly in little gasps, then moving down over him hungrily, biting into his arm, along his stomach, his legs, then shouting joyfully, moving up closer under him, her mouth wide open, his bearing down, his whole body shuddering.

Then she squeezed up alongside him, turning suddenly, bringing him down over her, her legs twisting around, her breath choking, her arms up, catching, bringing him into her, then bursting into moans and cries and shouts, tearing at his back with her nails, throwing herself up greedily to meet his body. He moved, kept moving, tried hard to move, not really feeling anything, just bewildered, frightened by what she was doing, might do, thinking only of what might happen if he should get tired and fall asleep there, and she still awake. And when he finally stopped moving, exhausted, she started retching, gasping, as if dying, then suddenly began laughing, crying, shouting, everything edged, vibrating, echoing nervously in the darkness around him. "You *are*, you *are* a young god! And I must have you always! Must devour you!"

He had jumped out of the bed, trying desperately to find the lights, and when he finally switched them on, she was lying in front of him, her flesh old and scarred. She cried out no, the skin by her arms hanging. Then became hysterical, her face twisting, shrieking out wildly, the energy just swooping down all around him, very close, thick. He didn't know what to do.

[161]

But swung suddenly. As if like something he had seen in a movie, thinking it would stop it, stop her, knock her out. Yet succeeding only in splitting her lower lip wide open. Then watching her sit there, like some crestfallen old owl hunching up, the blood spurting from her mouth, splattering out over him when she tried to speak. "You goddamn bastard! You goddamn bastard! You murderer!" Then cry as he bent closer to help her. Confused, scared. His first time. . . .

There was a tingling over his skin. Then against his beard. A smoothness filling out around him.

The girl hovering, her face above his; then her arms moved carefully up and around his neck, holding him in closer, her lips barely touching his.

He swallowed.

It was as if something had entered him.

Where or what he wasn't sure.

But gliding below the deep distrust, apprehension, of all that a woman might be.

There only a softness. Spreading out within. Warm, soothing. Very much the way a pebble drops in a pond, rings moving, one inside the other, no matter what had fallen there, a leaf, a pebble, a twig, whatever the shape, the ripple always the same, something unknown, trembling, set mysteriously alive on the water.

He breathed in deeply. Those rings spreading all through his body, curling down along his toes, then by the tips of his fingers, blending somehow with some as yet undiscovered side of himself, all the recesses of secrets there coming still closer. . . .

A WARMTH entered his lungs.

The girl turned.

Her nose grazing along his lips, tingling in the tiny crease at the side of his nostril.

Something formed, then came out, her shaking her head by the side of his cheek, the palm of her hand holding lightly against the other side of his face.

There was a very small sound. A sigh.

His touching her skin.

The ridge alongside, the little gully, smooth, soft, open.

Her legs stretching all the more around his, firm, warm, tilting in.

His hand slipping close by, her head, the rim of her ear, her ringlets.

Her body. His.

The warmth came back into him.

Then a scent, so well remembered, strong and sweet, passing through his nostrils into all the spaces of his head as though opening some secret pathway to what he was touching in her, as in all the wonder of those first few moments waking with someone, different parts meeting, limbs curling, uncurling, and then that smooth calm one feels rippling all along in the stillness of whoever else is emerging that says good morning as some state of enchantment whispering together in each other's body before anyone has even spoken or had the chance to stretch.

He moved his leg, around, over, her curling her hip up, the very center of their bones as if pressing tighter together, just rocking, warm, moist, something else as though loose belonging to both of them rolling back and forth inside, their holding all the more, trembling. . . .

Then she felt the pulse.

Inside her.

One, two . . .

She squeezed back.

Three.

The rhythm suddenly all through her.

Like a dance. Something moving between them. Slowly, mysteriously.

The pulse there again.

Tight, hard. Echoing from everywhere within her, reminding her of a poem she had once read, from Japan, of a wife who had made two little statues, one of herself, one of her husband, then crushed them together one night when he was home, re-forming them in that clay again, saying, "Now there's something of me in you, and something of you in me."

She curled and uncurled her toes.

Three. . . .

He heard the breathing.

Then felt the small quivering, the slight shifting of her weight.

Her face just above him in the darkness, her lips barely touching his.

It was only one moment.

One he no longer knew how to measure.

Only the rhythm of his heart filling in between his breath.

The rapidness of hers.

Their both trembling.

Those rings there even more, round, drawing out, one in the other, like one word spoken at the same time, the edge of its echo radiating all through him, between them, everything else still, the world seeming somehow to pause.

Then when it returned he could sense his weight, hers, moving through each other all the more, pulsing as if emanating from one point in the darkness. Like what he had seen but never understood, how all those Indian love statues balance in their positions, more a compass of embraces, all drawn together, linked always in the hub of their waists as though it were some ground, a center of gravity from which all the rest of the world takes its shape, its poise, if only one lets it come.

His breath held.

Everything becoming darker.

His realizing what was there.

Barely touching, waiting.

Its presence coming closer.

Her offering him a world.

Something strangely soulful, spirited, divine.

From wherever.

Very deep, longing.

Ready to unfold in all the depth of whatever to be shared.

Her stomach, her arms, her face, her lips pressing in gently. Against his.

His lips rising. Their meeting again. Cooler. Then resting.

Those rings all around him again, spreading softly, slowly, lingering through the bounds of their embrace.

An airy, floating sensation went through him.

He pressed his fingers deeper into the ringlets of her hair.

Her body beckoning, softly, lightly, the sweetness of its smell.

Her skin very warm, shadowy, flickering all along his.

Her breath coming into him, filling, then moving back slowly, what he had never imagined a kiss could be.

Their breathing together, the delicate rush of one causing the other's to bend and flicker, then grow larger, finer, like two long candle flames side by side.

A flutter went through him.

As though learning to talk on flows of feeling.

Everything becoming languorous with unsaid things.

He still inside her, her lips by his.

The ribbon of air coming into his lungs again, rising, falling gently, very moist, warm, tickling the top of his mouth and tingling down to the bottom of his body.

He remembered the silky ribbons dangling down before, the cloth of that upper chamber he had passed through bringing his body out in a way he scarcely knew, there now seeming another face rising within him, so different from the face he had known all his life, this one forming so quietly in the privacy of a kiss.

It suddenly reminding him of a man who had appeared once so deep in the jungle who the guides said had sat in a tree for most of the war catching leaves so that bombs would no longer fall, then coming down one day his body hunched,

[166]

his hair straggled, bits of leaves still stuck to his skin, all naked, everyone laughing, surprised, amazed, never having seen a holy man before, saying what a nut, a crazy coot, bananas, easing the tension only for a spell in how strange it seemed, then asking aren't you cold at night, his answering is your face cold, no, I'm all face, then walking off, bent from having sat so long, yet his foot sure, his eyes the same, bits of leaves stuck to his skin, everything so very quiet, everyone afraid to laugh.

He felt her fingers caress his face, her hand bringing a breeze closer to him like some first new breath.

An eyebrow emerged.

He kissed the moist, tiny thumbprint space at the base of her throat.

The tip of her tongue tingled across the top of his eyelash.

A strange billowy glow left behind, his moving his foot, gliding it over the smoothness, the warmth, the firmness, snuggling down along the curve of hers as her breath came back into him.

A long, rich "*oooh...*" seemed to sink in, echoing low and wide and endless all through the layers of his emotions, transforming all the pains there into some delicate spell, letting him feel quiet waves of "Oh, my God...oh my God ...oh..." rocking, flowing through him for the very first time.

Very much aware of their just lying there, joined together, some strange wishbone in a much deeper darkness than he had ever suspected, their bodies vibrating, their breath blending, embodying, forming, all those words unspoken like wishes just beginning.

Then their bodies curving tight to hold it all there, lapping softly, suddenly so beautiful, burning in bodies so much the same, a man, a woman, at the mouth of a cave in a world of startles for at least a million years, their making love so unchanged, the darkness there long before anything else was known, their holding closer with flickers on the wall, only the shadows of moons and stars along their skin winding like

[167]

recesses going deeper, with nowhere to begin or end, except on mysteries rising, all so tender, gentle, close.

He felt her breath float out over him.

His neck turning, loose.

Her chin curled closer to the tip of her shoulder. His hand around her back, his thumb slipping down suddenly into the opening formed between her cheek and shoulder, pearly dry, smooth, her whole body quivering.

Her lips moving in quickly to kiss his thumb, her shoulder adjusting, her breath very warm, moist, then cool through the hair of his chest.

He squeezed her, all the silent words mingling between them like some ancient awe forming in the hush of her skin with what he had never said yet longed for, holding her closer, his lips moving against hers, ". . .oh my darling. . .my dearest darling. . . ," her trembling even more.

Then she felt it.

There.

Rising so softly.

Flowing all the way back.

His bringing it up to her.

All through her.

Her cheek by his.

Everything strong, hidden, holding.

Yet like tiny fingertips pressing inside lightly.

With a murmur of a thousand tiny leaves.

Her legs as if dancing on their own, tapping down.

Trembling, with all that was coming into her, seeming ever so headless.

Like the golden blue deep within that famous grotto swimming up closer.

Her whole body as though a veil fluttering, some deeper breath whispering back warm.

Her cheek suddenly shaking, her neck tight with what was coming up.

Rising so quietly, so slow, so full, so warm.

And nothing there to fly, her body shuddering only to stay longer.

All aglow, as with those candles on some Easter walkway flowing down like a peacock's tail.

Holding back for all he would bring.

Filling places she never even knew could be there.

Then dropping back, catching quickly, all the lights suddenly flaming on the end of that tail.

Her breathing out breaths that were not breathing at all.

But heaving only to come back into him, within his arms, his chest, his muscles.

Held firm, tight, yet free to let herself go.

Folding over, becoming something else within that other space.

Mingling with all he was bringing still, ever so gently, tenderly, slow.

His chest rising, then pulling back.

Those rings suddenly there again.

His making room for them to breathe.

Knowing it was not a world she had offered.

But only herself in all she had left behind.

Her body very strong, defiant, close, like some ancient figurine.

Making his own cheeks glow so freely in how much they could care.

All his inner strength rushing up on waves of what a heart is thought to be.

Yet only some enchantment of a vow spreading through a burst of joy.

To let him offer himself within the spell of another kinship forming, some choice.

Very simple, pure.

His seeming to touch ground.

Settling. Coming. Quietly.

His heart beating.
Her cheeks.
His.
Her lips.
His squeezing harder.
Her heart forming deeper within rings that only seemed to smile.

"Hello. . .
. . .my woman. . . ."

He felt the tear drop.

"Hi. . .
. . .my man. . . ."

Something suddenly spreading even sweeter from the darkness above him.
So very delicious.
Tender, soft, holding.
As though children forming within the magic of those rings.
His shoulders never seeming so broad, strong.
For all that was so light.
Little bodies so close.
Saying, *See. . .see. . .see. . .*
Belonging, human.
And something else so much deeper, older, wiser, answering.
Yes. . .yes. . .see. . .see. . . .isn't it all wonderful. . .so very special. . .see. . . .
All the twinkling there.
His blowing on it carefully with what was still echoing within him.
Both children bouncing.

[170]

Each on a different shoulder.
Close, held together, brothers.
Looking in different ways.
All the stars surrounding them.
And his just saying, feeling as a father, *ah. . .my. . .oh.
. .yes. . .all so many things. . .isn't it lovely. . .it all so special.
. .and you both so special. . .with all the different things you
can see. . . .*

He could feel the tear sparkling in his own eye.
Her face above him in the darkness.
So very close.
Her lips, touching, untouching.
Like a butterfly.
Their kiss, its wings.
Their bodies, new worlds moving by.
Quiet, alive, alone.

". . .Hi. . ."

"WHERE ARE YOU?"
The old voice suddenly cut through the darkness.
The lights switching on.

Then there was a bang. A thud. A crash.
Everything collapsing.
Their falling.
His rolling out into something jamming down.
Something else cutting up against his cheek.

All the lights blinding.

The crests of her voice still ringing in the air, his not knowing what she had cried out, nor where she might be.

His elbows hit the ground. He quickly began crawling, pushing up behind something, his breath scorching as though flames were all around him, yet all the sounds, noises, other voices, thunder, coming as if from under water, drawing out, whining, bursting, hitting from all sides at once. Only a blinding pain piercing deeper into the back of his eyes, blowing out blotches in front like some burning visual wind, red, raw, blistering, then sticking onto him, yellow and green and white.

He tried to catch his breath, biting down on his tongue, reaching out, the colors still swirling out before him like a jumble of tattoos, his uncertain where to move, where to find her, groping along the ground among the scatter of things, not recognizing any pattern by which to find his way, as though lost again deep in some enemy land in the blinding of the light.

He started inching automatically, listening carefully, not knowing what had happened, the crests of her voice still ringing in his ears, becoming faint, distant, coming from nowhere that he knew, yet somehow close. Then it was quiet. A hush. A pause. Suddenly becoming aware of the blood trickling over his body from the gash along his cheek. Sticky, warm. And some other presence close to him, like a huge shadow beyond all the light that he could just barely sense, gliding along him, over him, his arms, his chest, his legs.

It startled him. He crawled forward quickly, squeezing under something, keeping his shoulder against a wall, the lights stronger, blinding again whenever he came up against an opening, his fingers scratching quickly around the rubble, shards, pieces, not knowing what he was up against, burrowing down into an edge, coming up somewhere else, colors still

streaking out in front of him, long, red, blue, his hands
clutching onto a bar, pulling himself up, then falling over
against the ground, the dirt, the coarseness, the bits and
pieces, the stringy things, the cloth, the stones, pebbles, sticks,
nothing making any sense.

He just kept moving ahead, feeling things out there that
were brushing by, leading him on. Then his arms banged into
a wicker lattice shorn up as a wall or some kind of grating or
trap in front of him. He grabbed hold of it, hanging there,
trying to calm himself, pressures moving inside him as though
stuck down at the back of his throat. Images forming.
Shadowy. Vague lines before him in the burning of the light.
Feeling he were at that rubber wall again, pressing through,
trying to reach beyond, the tip of his forehead up against the
coldness of it. A terrible premonition of what was in store for
him. He felt dazed. Memories forming.

A sinking pain came back tugging all through him.

Remembering those old hands. In his room. Pressing up
against his. Not knowing who had come in. The bird inside.
The featheriness warm, pulsing. The skin of those hands so
very strange, like a ripe soft fig just beginning to dry. Hearing
the aspirate whisper saying, *"Mea culpa, mea culpa."* Then
the hands just squeezing, prayer-like, the throbbing inside
louder, aching, the bird trying to bite its way out. The soft old
hands only tightening, the tiny rib cage snapping, the flutter
of heat, struggling against his palms, his head pounding,
bringing everything back, the beak sticking deeper up into his
skin, quivering there before it stayed still.

He could see the face again. Not realizing really who it
might be, the first time there. Puffy, old, the whitish,
yellowish hair, the cheeks almost cherubic, heavy creases all
along the forehead, a tired smile held more for fear of falling,
the eyes odd, sheepish, yet glistening, and that strangely
courteous, patronizing tone in the old voice as when other
urgent things have been on one's mind for a long time, as yet

[175]

unresolved, but are still pressing, waiting, needing something special, only half revealed.

"I take it you saw the bulletin. I've been fortunate, you know, how I made my money. Well, it's just my little way of doing something. The boardinghouse some small way of giving it back. Not much else you can do with things, buy, sell, scrap, store them, change them, pass them on, give them new names. Wouldn't you agree? So unlike things of the spirit."

The little smile, the tone, changing, waiting, swelling slightly, an odd enticement there, a little laugh, the one cocked eye going out strangely, giving the uncomfortable feeling of being watched from somewhere else.

"True, the neighborhood's a little bad now, I know, but all our memories are here. Besides, somehow there always seems more space to the abode of old downtown wealth, so easy to divide up, do with as you like, without much notice, concern, restrictions. Quite different from where I had to go to make it. Absolutely nothing there." A pause. The waiting again. Then the tone half with pride, half with a raspiness underneath, as from being about to tell the same story over again, the eyes looking away, reminiscing, yet more to hold him there till their attention returned. "Small Central-American towns. Setting up factories. All over out in the sticks. The help unbelievably cheap, working for nothing, then of all things stopping in a week, with enough to live for the rest of the year, the way they wanted to live. An incredible disaster." The old hands going up, holding there. "Well, would you believe, all solved by mail-order catalogs? Just giving them away by the carload. Everybody going back to work. Hardly ever going home. It not the apple afterall, my friend, it only Sears Roebuck. For today." The smile wide, the tone preening, more at ease, the hands going to his chest. "Of course I got nothing from that, you understand. But then I made the biggest discovery of my life, which let me have the finer

[176]

things, and teaches you the value of knowing even the most minute details. Just some old Civil War tariff. On freight. For shipping biscuits. To the army. Not much of a saving over other bakery goods, mind you, but it would add up, I knew. Showing you the value of the fallout from such wars. So, many years ago, I went to the largest cookie company and said, 'Look, I can save you a fortune each year for a small percentage if you're willing to take the risk and have faith in me before I let you know how.' They took the risk. Faith always based on great expectations. It made me very comfortable. And they simply changed their name, becoming a major biscuit company. Allowing me to devote myself to the arts, the mind, the soul." He smiled very wide, turning slightly in the chair, the hands outstretched again. "Well, if you allow, I think I have just the place for you, so let me help you settle in with your things, you don't know how pleased I am to have you here, it's so rare there are others than just students who come, and I can make any of the arrangements you need, no matter what, I'm really very happy to help, and very anxious to learn in detail just what it is you are working on, it all seems so exciting, so baffling, challenging. My daughter will assist you in any way she can, she's a big help, quite frankly at my age I rely on her myself, she's very dear to me, one always expects a son, at least in my times, girls a bit of a surprise, so hard to raise, finding their potential, and then so hard to give up later, unless, well, fathers can be jealous about those things. . . . Yes. Well, come now, let me take you up to where you'll be. . . ."

He felt the draft stealing into him again, moving down through his limbs and chest, its presence, shadowy, vague, foreboding. His forehead still tipped up against the coldness, his arms hanging out, an ominous swooshing sound outside. His swallowing harder. The images clearing, shaping out, his eyes trying desperately to adjust to detach himself, but colors only swirling around them, connecting up, more like memories meshing from how deep he had been before he could make out what was really in front of him.

That terrible sinking feeling still going through him, his remembering the swoosh of pigeons flying across the window in the hospital. Then his father just-sitting there in a green robe after his stroke, shoulders hunched, eyes dull, shuffling whenever he walked, barely talking anymore. Those quiet moments with so much wanting to be said. "You had a great gift. I don't understand. You abused it. Even more than your voice." Then hesitating, seeing the film over those eyes, adding quickly, changing, touching him, "You just didn't take care of yourself, Dad." Hearing another swoosh of pigeons outside along the wall. "For all of us. As we all would have liked you to. Just being a father." The pause, the look, all the lines along the face. "What else could I have done?" The voice croaked. That moment so quiet. Then the sigh. "I saw there was a chance." "What for?" "For everything, just everything." "Well. . . ." Then the pause. Endless. A shoulder poised only slightly higher, it all seeming so isolated, simply a quiet caving in, even illness not contagious anymore. Then his just folding his hands, thinking of those flickers in Plato's cave, nothing really out there, everything blind, everyone blind to each other, with all the promises, only shudders left groping in all that darkness, whatever it was behind a face. . . .

He pulled back quickly. Finding the wall again. Pressing his knuckles down deep on the ground by it until he could feel the pain spreading up through his arms blocking out what was coming over him, then crawling along, the wall becoming broad, smooth, damp, curving out, then beginning to pocket back, the end dead, like a *cul de sac*, only throwing him back on himself. He stopped. Then he suddenly heard the other voices. Recognizing them. Not knowing where they were coming from.

He lay very flat, his stomach stretched out along the dirt,

[178]

his fingers curling in, the dust going in dry through his nostrils, his holding his breath to keep from choking, then turning over, the warmth of the light all along his body, his staring up, not moving, the cuts along his cheek and body burning, the blood caking, the dirt gritting in his mouth against his teeth. *One, two, three.*

Remembering his big brother's face, round, open, smiling, peering over the top of his bunk bed, looking down, having made a little elevator machine with a box and some string wrapped around an empty spool attached to the post, his lowering the little box, saying *here she comes,* making a whirring noise, then asking him to play too, putting his candy and stuff into it, hoisting it back up, always beckoning for him to count out more, nothing ever coming back down, his just counting, *one, two, three,* his brother getting sick, with all those chills and fevers, staying in bed for a very long time, and his having to sleep in the living room then, drawing pictures on the windows when he was lonely, the windows always steaming up, the night very dark, and his playing with himself by asking what all the first ten numbers would add up to, leaning over the back of the sofa, drawing on the window with his finger, running out of space, then erasing it, blowing back on the glass to steam it up so he could keep adding, and suddenly thinking of an easier way, erasing everything with his pajama sleeve, putting down the first five numbers in a line and for some reason reversing them in another line underneath, *five, four, three, two, one,* and noting that each column added up to six, which was only one more than the whole amount, which was half of the original ten, his realizing in awe while his finger was curled cold and wet that whatever number he were to choose, the number plus one times half the number would yield the sum of all the numbers within it, his finger up against the glass becoming very warm, then his whole body flushing, warm, cold, trembling with his discovery, all the excitement, and his enjoying it, not understanding what it all meant, not knowing what to do with all that he was feeling, and then those looks he always got from his mother, when daydreaming about what numbers could do or when she first said *will you please hurry!* and he answered *why, it's not raining?*, then all the yelling, talking to teachers, where his mind was half the times, his mother only glaring, his father unconcerned, then putting his head down that one night, running with all his might, smashing up into the curving glass brick wall in the dining room, all the sound, the cry, the lights, blood over the floor, his parents upset by all his awkwardness, *for christsakes why didn't you put the lights on if you had to go to the bathroom, dummy, can't you walk right*, his eyes wide open, tears trickling over his cheeks, seeing all the stars, just juggling, going up into each other, staying there, making funny faces, becoming different things, passing through one another like rainbows of shapes and blurs with all the colors Columbus must have seen when he first came to land wondering if it were spumoni, all the different colored faces, his suddenly really liking whatever kind of mind he had, however much it hurt, thinking of all the neat and wonderful things it could do, could create in the darkness, glad it had not gone away afterall.

He closed his eyes, turning back over. He saw those blue eyes again. So bright. So shiny. So unreal. Moving downward under the golden hair, flickering ever so quickly to the side, casting the glow of another world the way a tip of a tongue can dart so swiftly to moisten the corner of one's mouth.

"It's only the romance they want you for, no matter what you look like," his brother speaking on the secrets of women, "it's just that simple, give them that, you get them, all cunts in the dark are the same. And when the romance is over, or you're not doing enough to surprise them, bringing flowers, putting an aspirin in the water so they last longer, reminding them all the more when you're not there, you start finding bits of toilet paper between their crack, if you even get that far, if they haven't got some other sucker around already. Let me tell ya, now that you're getting bigger," his brother went on, waxing on the ways of life, "scoring and keeping other dudes out is a tough business, and romance is the name of the game."

His remembering his brother coming home from a date with a quiet, mousy little girl once who wouldn't put out, his storming into the house switching on the lights in their room late at night, yelling, "shit, shit, shit," waking him up to have an audience, then walking around the bedroom, knocking into things, mumbling, "fucking little whore, little cunt, bitch," pulling off his clothes, glowering, saying, "just wait, just wait," ending up putting his fist through the hollow veneer of their bedroom door, their mother coming out quickly from her room, screaming, "Oh my God, what happened, what happened?" his brother only answering that he was in an accident, no one hurt, the car just a little smashed up, finally getting her to go back to bed, while he sat down on his bed still fuming, "little cunt, smart-ass little cunt, goddamn it, bitch, wait!" Then taking her out more till he realized that she just didn't put out for a long while, whether or not for him, then deciding to marry her, knowing how long it would take others. "She's O.K., nice, sweet, we're not in love, but for what I'm going to do, someone is always going to try to make my wife, and I know I've got three months' insurance. And believe me I tried everything to turn her on, so she'll be good for me."

Bringing back only that other time, his brother's eyes aglow, standing with him in the museum in front of the glass case that held the gold and enamel Cellini cup with its fluted shell resting on the wings of a griffin all held on the back of a tortoise. "Someday I'll have that." "But if it's in a museum, how?" "Listen, in this country nothing is just given to you, whatever you want has to be taken, and today anything is possible, anything." "Yeah, but you can just come and see it whenever you want." "Ah yes, but so can others. You really

[181]

have no practical sense, you know. What you want is only worth more if others want it too and don't have it, and those things are priceless, one of a kind, because no one else can ever have it but you. That's what the race is for. A winner. *Numero uno.* Ergo, the Cellini Cup." His eyes magnificently, yet feverishly aglow, covetous in the presence of what was for him the ultimate trophy for all his ambitions, so reminiscent of the Ovaltine cup with the picture of the funny little turtle with the world on his back that his mother would always bring in to him to say good night when he was sick in bed and that so much later he was to make the emblem of all his companies, putting the picture on the tail of his plane, as if holding together all the contradictions in him in whatever the secret bond between the sympathy so craved, and the success so needed, and all the risks he would have to take to have both.

"Someday. Someday. And when I have that," his face puffing up, self-made, "we'll be beyond it all, believe me. . . ."

A spasm went through him. His swallowing. The sand scratchy, dry, all along his throat. Then he opened his eyes. It darker in the dirt. Like the first time he had put that blindfold on, the shells, the cotton, lying in bed, waiting to wake up that way, seeing his wife's face fixed before him, very clear and sharp, as though eternal, drifting away like a decal. Now his brother's. Hers. Slipping off together into whatever world of their own. Crisp, irrevocable, foreign. . . .

"Jesus, what the fuck is it in here, it's like a pigsty!"
"Look, there he is."
"Shit, he's stark naked."
"Oh my God. . . ." The eyes.
"See, see, fuck, I knew it, I knew it, look at him, he is crazy, crazy!"

He moved out quickly, all the training coming back, his elbows digging in, that smell there, other things banging,

[182]

turning over, knocking, crashing, his not telling how near, how far, everything else milky, his wanting the darkness again, needing some guide. He reached out against the wall, slapping with the flat of his hand, then leaned closer, sliding along with his ear, beginning to crawl more rapidly along with the cold. It became warmer, plastery, then an edge. He ran his fingers along it: beyond, up higher, was a crack, then an opening breaking through. He remembered where he was.

He scaled up into it, his arms tight against the sides. It was cooler, darker. He passed under something heavy and soft, swelling back over him. On the other side was a smooth ceramic ledge that curved inward like a duct of some kind, his knowing it would take him around to the side where he wouldn't be expected. He angled onto it, the cool hardness flattening his palms and knees; he could feel the trembling in his hands, trying to keep themselves light and ready. He kept moving up, around, then came down slowly, very quietly, inching onto the dirt in front of him. He could still feel things—concrete, calculated, there, shaped against his hands— no matter how or where he moved now, as though scaling a cliff or staying close to the rocks or ground shrubs. His timing back, a swell of excitement, the energy suddenly pouring into him, the ground moving out. He felt high, tense, alive.

He saw the dim figure standing out in front of him. The jacket, the roundness.

He stopped.

Crouching low.

Breathing heavily.

His biceps flexing slowly, rhythmically, pulsing at the warmth of his arms.

His beard scratchy, hot, on his chest, as though he were becoming something else, more primitive, at the center of things, a quarry waiting.

He just held still. He could feel the breeze riffling over him, barely funnelling through the slight air space his biceps were leaving against the arm skin, opening and closing, like a mouth, the thin film of sweat evaporating, signalling the directions of any change in the air. A quiet, new exhilaration went through him.

Only an instant. *If. . .then. . . .* His own arms shooting up abruptly, moving down against the thick muscles at the inset of the neck, grabbing into the soft part of the throat, reaching in, or changing quickly to slide the palm of his hand up, fingers curving down, ready for the eyes instead, his other hand pressing against the collarbone, or bringing the back of his hand down back against the neck, cracking it.

His fingers curling in the dirt. The draft coming back. Moist, clammy. That smell around him. The figure still standing in front of him. His groping out, crawling very quietly. The tips of his fingers sensing the sharpness, the sand, the curves moving in and along the edges or stones. His hands burning, tingling. His fingers closing, unclosing. The dirt becoming soft, talcy, smoothing around them. A very small pebble moving against them. Rolling between, playing around his fingertips. Soothing, elusive. Like the little spoon, the bevels, the lines, the curves, the hollows for eyes, the little ugly face, beckoning, moving inside him, the tiny ripple of those cherubic cheeks, soothing. He closed his eyes. Holding still.

A strange hush there. That chalky, eerie sensation going through him again. His fingertips playing around the pebble. His suddenly aware of his touching it, its touching him, pressing quickly back and forth, the two feelings overlapping, yet so different. One, silky, smooth, the other cold, hard. Like opposites fitting together, blending almost, as though every touching were two, forgotten, disguised, belonging really to no one, so very quiet and unspoken.

He held his breath. A low, barely perceptible hum washing over him like the inside of a clam shell sounding softly against his skin. His body tingled. His fingers reaching in. His shuddering. Remembering the sudden catch, the deep swallowing, the poppling, the knot loosening, tightening, playing in a vibrato against his fingers like some sort of strange bond. The sensation of blood and cold in his nostrils, the kind that comes on a wintry day, penetrating, brisk, so much lighter, clearer, in all that inner shaking. And then that other softness, silky, smooth, misty, almost less a contact than a presence, her fingers curling round, the cup of tea, the special flush in her skin, its warmth seeming to close over the slight space between them. His body quivered.

The hum became stronger. His skin stretching out all along him, growing taut. He sensed something rippling in the air around him, like that of a cavern, cool, thin, unopened. He began crawling cautiously, somehow feeling where he should go again by the instep along his back, his shoulder blades moving one against the other, rubbing, warming.

That draft came back. Cool, moist, then becoming smoother, softer, warmer, opening more, a presence all around, passing by him like the balm of a summer's day.

He swallowed. A tiny rivulet of air catching up with what he had felt before, what had come inside, so unspoken, yet going so deep into him, through him, away from him. He felt he was moving up and down very slowly through himself, some somersault on a rivulet of air as strange as the way water drops down colder, until, like some odd clock, it changes, expanding, rising in a new way, floating up from the solid ice it would have become so long ago had that mysterious degree never been found, the moment that nothing ever could have predicted counting down, somehow keeping it alive.

A pang of homesickness shot through him.

He kept rubbing the pebble back and forth between his fingers.

There was an odd sound.

Like the dull, quick inner spunk of some wick lighting.

That other darkness inside seeming to spread out, contouring, shaping, changing. As if up against everything and yet below it.

[185]

Making his body so very deep, ghostly.

As though everything were suspended for a moment.

His skin, his muscles, all too tired, too exhausted, to move anymore.

Then he could feel it.

Simple. Small. By itself.

Not because of anything, but just there, coming from nowhere. Beyond all the training. Flickering. Like a fine feather flame. Deep within himself where he was still breathing cool.

It so rarified. Not even like the claustrophobia. His understanding now in the way he was breathing why people were so terrified of blindness. There was almost nothing. But around that odd glowing he could feel things that were even less. Unearthly. Empty. More ghostly. With really no space, no walls, no containers, and yet everything. As if slung over hollows of primitive marrow bones with their endless, empty chambers sinking deeper, the stillness echoing, sounding softly, going further, what the old must know instinctively about illness, those moments they want so desperately to talk about again and again, trying to get down to those sources, those still earlier energy pools, edging along the hollows of how they feel, sinking down in the darkness of that interior, there no longer any clues, only the need to re-discover something on its own, pure, then its suddenly spunking, edging off the panic that's always there, like the fear, the pain in one's body, wearing in, glowing softly, deeply, wafting with some other blessing there, a holiness within, its consciousness rising, so rarefied in that other world, its secrets lost, or never really known, what all the pilgrims, explorers, pioneers were searching for all along, a spark, that flame, coming where nothing else was, to let it glow, burn, thinking it was some frontier, some unending, unimaginable space, rather than just one mysterious point from which their efforts came, what they had inside all along, so very unreal, human, alive.

He felt the awe.

[186]

There was another flame. Flickering all along his.

Touching, untouching.

The delicate rush of one causing the other to bend and flicker, then grow finer, larger, side by side.

A flutter went through him.

Sensing that soft skin so elusively all around him, turning slowly, pulsing, warm, misty, a long delicate thread dropping into whatever labyrinth, in all that was feminine within him salted away like tears lest it seem unmanly, now stirring in that darkness, moving up unsaid on flows of feeling.

He shuddered.

But very slow, gentle, tender.

As though a shudder still some vestige of intimacy.

Breaking through whatever side of himself so carefully hidden.

Neither selfish nor selfless, but a union flickering quietly, side by side, long flames coming closer, bending, swirling, with all the glow of dreams, of memories, bringing together all that is noble, lofty, human, between the two.

He was rising.

His heart beating faster.

Feelings forming, blending, changing.

A sweet scent of fruit there, heady, soothing, as in some fine day.

His moving slowly.

There like bulrushes all along the sides. Going through him.

Long. Hollow. Deep. Brushing aside, swaying back slowly. Nodding their heads. Marshy.

Then veils. Pulling back inside. Fluttering, breezy. Drooping down. Billowing back from under. Clouds drifting by. The swirls inside wispy. Very light, pithy. Rings in the water.

A strange breath. Very close. Hovering. Fluttering. An uprooted tree. Rings around it, leaves floating, never moving. A white-necked duck drifting, swirling around, the taupe female, bottom feathers fluttering, flowing this way, that,

[187]

treading, moving the other way around, all along the sides, its drake there, underwater clues webbing against their feet, staying closer, heads nodding from beneath the toes, all through the rings, barely parting.

Rushes moving by, the sedge bending, bamboo waving, a breath letting out. Flowing back into gullies. Marshy cattails, cork trees, roots exposed. The narrow ribbons, jutting out, fingery. Black mud holes. Crayfish scurrying back, waving their large claws. The water flowing away, frothy. Twigs touching.

The rings changing, becoming other things, no longer a ring rising. A pebble dropping. The water foggy. A duck raising its wings, flapping the breeze, then sinking down, its small tail feathers waving. Fingery, soft. Everything parting. Glistening.

A sail opening. Luffing. Fluttering. Another breeze blowing gently. The sail popping. Other voices there. Songs. So different from the ones at home. Another kind of people. Different-colored faces. Another couple, yellow skin, however faraway. Like ones he had killed. Yet still alive. Holding their breath in a folk song for what they can no longer say. The words still there, hidden, old, glistening, for all mankind:

I see a banner fly.
Atop the village pole.
The old man humming in the night.
With sounds of songs flying to us all.
Hope. Yearn for. Remember. Love.

"Hey, there he is."

"Hey stop!"

"Jesus, fuck, will you hurry and get him before everyone else sees him and it's in all the goddamn papers!"

"Stop, will you!"

"Listen to them, for christsakes."

"...No...Stop...Don't...Leave him...," the old voice called out. "Let him be."

There was a whistling over his head.
A breeze all along his body.
He jumped up. His mouth opening.
There were suddenly a thousand tiny leaves.
Winds blowing in different directions.
A labyrinth, all, always.
Whether summer, winter, spring, fall.
In some funny face of love all around him.
"*I love you,*" he whispered, "*wherever, whenever.*"

His coming back down. Happy.
Hopping on one foot, then the other.
Moving off quickly.
Disappearing.
Before they could reach him.

"Which way did he go?"
"Around the bend."
"Ah, shit!"
"Crazy asshole!"
"Go back, check the girl, see what he's done to her."
"Alright."
"Never mind, hurry and get him!"
"Yeah, c'mon."
"Move it."
"Let's go."

"*And I do you. . .whenever, wherever. . . .*"

The sounds still ringing softly on the air.

"*. . .Hi. . .*"

"*. . .Hello. . .*"